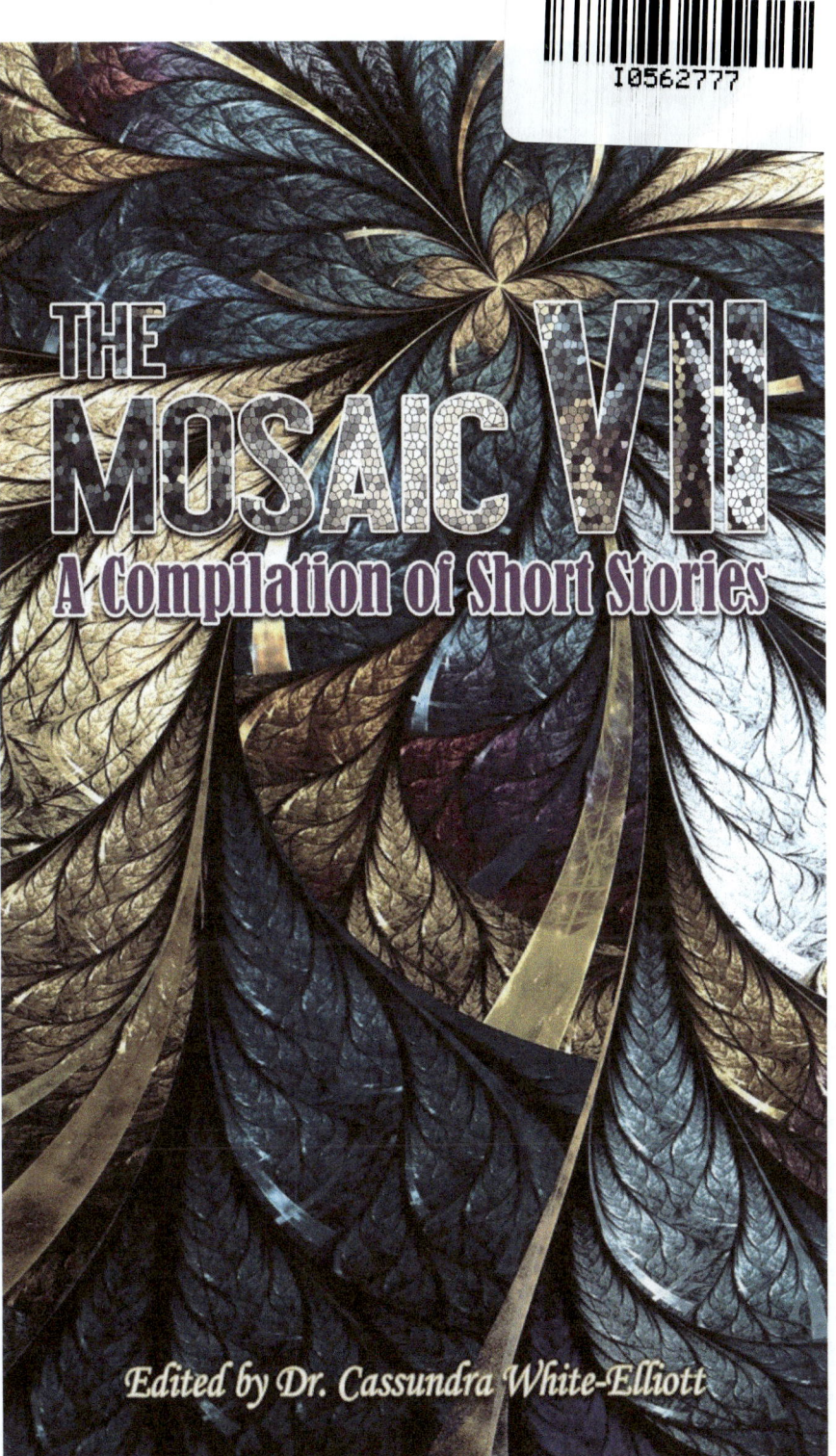

THE MOSAIC VII

A Compilation of Short Stories

Edited by Dr. Cassundra White-Elliott

This book contains works of both non-fiction and fiction. In the cases of fictional writings, the stories may have been fashioned after true stories but are not exact retellings.

CLF Publishing, LLC.
www.clfpublishing.org

Cover design by Senir Design. Contact information: info@senirdesign.com.

ISBN # 978-1-945102-35-6

Printed in the United States of America.

Dedications

This book is dedicated to all aspiring writers who were told they couldn't make it in the field of writing or who may have been too scared to move forward because of a fear of failure.

The writers, whose stories are included within, are proof that you can be successful and your dreams can be a reality.

So, I invite you to pursue your own writing and be the success you know you are.

Dr. Cassundra White-Elliott

Acknowledgements

I acknowledge all the participants in this project, who helped to see it from its stages of inception to its complete fruition.

May your success be plentiful, as you continue to pursue your educational and writing endeavors. I look forward to working with each of you individually, collectively, or both, in the near future.

Much love and appreciation,

C. White-Elliott

Dr. Cassundra White-Elliott

Table of Contents

Introduction

Welcome to **The Mosaic VII**, where you will enter the exciting world of short stories. Here, the imagination can and will unfold right before your very eyes. What you least expect just may become the expected.

The seventeen authors have delved within their own imaginations and pulled out all the stops and barred no holds. Their tales will excite you, cause curiosity to grow, bring tears of sadness, and/or even feelings of wonderment.

They are skillful in their craft, and they are to be congratulated for their efforts. They have stepped into unknown territory with publishing and sharing their talents with the world at large.

So, I invite you to sit back, relax with your favorite drink, curl up in your most comfortable chair and be prepared for the journeys that lie ahead.

With no further ado, I invite you to ENJOY!!!!!!!!!!

Edited by Dr. C. White-Elliott

Someone I Never Knew

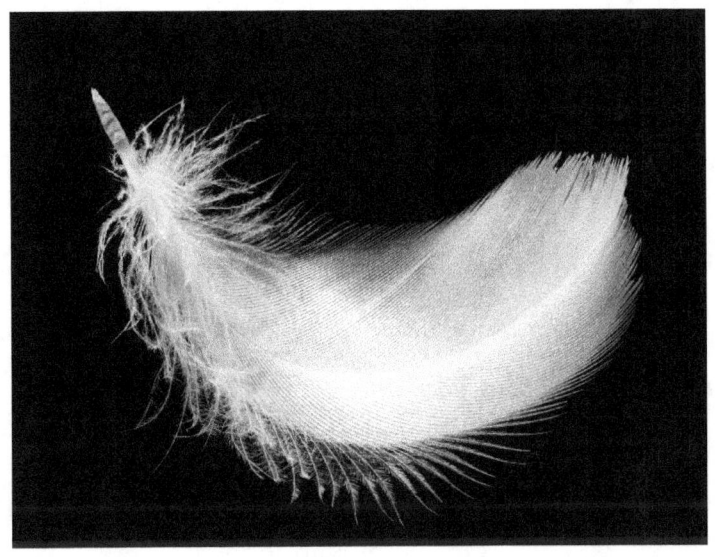

Naimi Alvarado

"Beware; for I am fearless, and therefore powerful."

Frankenstein- Mary Wollstonecraft Shelley

"...I've made many and plenty mistakes in my life. I have many faults, and I have many more fears, but I'm gonna embrace myself as hard as I can, and I'm starting to love myself gradually just little by little..."

BTS- Kim Namjoon

May has had an easy life. Sure, there have been some major traumas in her life, leading to her really low self-esteem and the belief that she has what she deserves, like the one time she was sent to the hospital by the hands of her ex-partner. But compared to others, she still had it easy, until now. One of the privileges she had was the comfort of being taken care of, financially speaking. Of course, there were times in her household when money was really tight but they always managed to survive; thus, her urgency to get a job was really low. Speaking of household, she has or had, no one knows at this point, a partner, a beautiful, big brown sparkly-eyed girl named Genesis, age eleven, and a dog. It was a small, perfect, and imperfect family.

April 2017 was the date that changed her life. I call that day-her awakening. She got a stable job, working five days a week, five or six hours a day. It was nothing much, but to her, it was refreshing. When money started to come, she started to realize she could do more. She realized she could be free, a feeling she did not know nor felt before, and she needed it. She fancied more; she craved accomplishments. May decided to go back to school. Being a simple worker was not and never would be enough, and so, she did. Her wings started to grow.

October 30, 2017 was the date of the downfall, the day she knew what hell felt like, the day she learned how to hate someone to the point of imagining a thousand ways to kill someone. It was the date I feared for her life, the day I saw her crumble, the day I saw her rise from the ashes like a phoenix, her rebirth.

It was a typical California day, hot in the day and cold at night. She went to work like any normal day. Her job was fine, and she was busy, happy, and content. Late in the afternoon, she got a phone call from a neighbor, telling her she needed to come back home because her partner did something and the issue needed to be addressed as soon as possible to avoid a major conflict. She told them she could not leave her job and ended the phone call. Around nine that evening, she got another phone call, but that time it was the police, letting her know her partner was taken to jail. Her daughter was home alone, and she needed to come home quickly. When she heard those words, the world became mute. She could not hear anything but the fast beating of her heart. She came back to her senses in a few seconds, and the next thing she felt was a fiery rage running through her veins. She was furious to whoever did that to her family. She was seeing red, and she was ready to kill. Then, she was a total wreck, down on the floor wailing. Then, she was still- petrified without a clue of what to do next. She was left all alone with little to no weapons to defend herself. It was a scary moment. It was so pitiful witnessing that part of her. Never in a hundred years would I have thought she would face such tragedy.

It has been a year already since the incident. She is still fighting for justice, still fighting for the truth, fighting for survival, fighting for her daughter, and sometimes fighting for herself. She is a little bit better now. The tears have stopped. She is still fearful, but at least, she is moving.

May is all alone. She does not have friends, family, or relatives of the sort. It is only her and her daughter. The closest thing she has as human interaction is with her coworkers.

Things have changed, May can see that; I cannot say if it is for better or for worse. I think it is too early to decide that. Her and her daughter's routine has made a one hundred and eighty degree turn. One of those changes is May working from ten to twelve hours a day; another is her lack of proper sleep, but that is not what bothers her. It is the fact that her daughter stays with her all the time. Like I said, she has no one to rely on to take care of Genesis when she works. Her daughter is now the one that has no friends outside of school, and that concerns her to no end. She is only eleven, and she spends six hours of her day confined to a little table, in the corner, like a scolded puppy, inside of a restaurant waiting for her mother to finish her work, and then she goes to bed way too late for a middle school girl. It is a heartbreaking scene.

May does not mind work all the time. She has to work even if she does not want to because someone depends on her. Now, all of the responsibilities weigh on her shoulders: the rent, bills, food, clothes, lawyers, paying back the money she borrowed from people that took pity on her, gasoline, school supplies, and the cherry on top of the cake- her non-resident tuition college fee that by the way is almost three thousand dollars. So, even if she does not want to go to work, she has to. How does she do it? I do not know.

I am starting to believe she uses her job as an excuse to not think about her biggest problem. She is a coward that much I know. She keeps on hiding underneath her job. Not only she is running away from the problem, but she has another big issue to resolve. But, that is a story for another time. She keeps tiring herself out just to be able to sleep a little bit better in the silent nights. She tires her brain and body, so she does not do any harm to herself. She hates herself. I am very aware of that, and I cannot do anything about it. She refuses to see what I see.

She refuses to love herself. She refuses to believe she is worth it. She refuses to believe she is doing an amazing job. She refuses to believe me, the one who has been with her all the time on the sidelines.

Despite the fact that the bubble she used to live was burst and the situation she was living in was tiring, painful, and frustrating, I could see a positive effect because I have seen the birth of someone I never knew. I have had the pleasure to see her grow. I have seen her become fearless, stronger, and driven. I know the road is long and tedious, and it will have its ups and downs. I know she would still believe she is not enough, not strong, but I can see her victorious. Now, she has me, and I will make sure to remind her every single day that she can do it. I will be on the sidelines cheering, "Keep going!"

Her only goal is to provide a good life for her daughter. She hopes to one day hear from her, "Thank you, Mommy, for not giving up." I know she is going to grow old to witness the metamorphosis of her precious little caterpillar into a magnificent butterfly. And then maybe, just maybe, she will finally say: "Yes, I was strong all along. I can sleep at ease now."

I hope to stay with her until that day.

About the Author

Naimi Alvarado in a Mexican native living in California. Her residency has been the city of Redlands for the last twelve years. She is pretty much in love with that city.

Currently, she is majoring in sign language at Crafton Hills College. She also has a full-time job and an eleven-year-old daughter. She likes to write, but she enjoys to read much more.

Daniel and the Craziest Welcome Home Party in History

https://www.dieepic.com

J.D. Delgado

"Keep your dreams alive. Understand to achieve anything requires faith and belief in yourself, vision, hard work, determination, and dedication. Remember, all things are possible for those who believe."

Gail Devers

It was a sunny and oven-like Monday morning. Daniel Blaze had no idea what to do. He was thinking about whether or not he really wanted to get out of bed that morning. "Screw it," he said to himself. He lifted himself from his bed. He was drenched in sweat, as if someone had poured water on his back. He could not sleep the night before because he couldn't stop thinking of his son Peter. He woke up with a sore neck. He must've had a violent nightmare because his bed sheets and pillows were all over his floor, as if he had thrown them from his bed.

Every day, he wished he could have his son back. But, there was no bringing him back from the dead. Daniel hated himself for not being there when his son had died. He also wished he had been there for his birthday. Daniel was stationed in Afghanistan with the U.S. Army as a Staff Sergeant. Daniel couldn't believe that he couldn't be home for the birth of his son; let alone the tragic death of his son. His son as far as he knew was seven years old and died of sudden unexpected death syndrome. When Daniel's son died, Jenna his wife of fifteen years had left him because she couldn't stand having to deal with the death of her firstborn without her husband there by her side.

When Daniel received the divorce papers, he couldn't believe it. The woman he loved was deciding to leave him. He

Dear Daniel,

I appreciate your love and caring words. I don't think that I can be with you if you are in the army. Unless you are here, I don't want to live a life where I am always wondering when you are going to come home. I have been going through a depression since Peter died weeks after you had to go back to base. If you love me, please come home.

Sincerely,

Jenna

didn't know how to handle it because she was his first love. Daniel decided that he would try to write her a letter, try to make amends, and try to convince her to stay with him. Months went by after Daniel sent the letter, and finally, he received a response from Jenna. The letter said:

Daniel had thought about the letter for a while. Daniel didn't know what to say. He decided he would ask his brothers in the army. His buddy Sev had said to add Handsome Manboy on Snapchat. Daniel asked why he should follow Shauniee Stylez. Sev looked at Daniel like he was crazy. Sev then replied, "Shauniee always has beautiful girls, funny stories, and great tips once in a while. He even invented the best coffee concoction ever!" Sev kept rambling on and on about Shauniee. Daniel figured he would just add Shauniee on Snapchat. Daniel waited some time and finally got his add-back on snapchat and decided to tell Shauniee about his situation. Daniel watched his story after his duties on the base were done.

Shauniee appreciated that someone in the military had contacted him for advice. Off the bat, Daniel could tell Shauniee was a down-to-earth and kind-hearted person because the first thing Shauniee said was to fight for Jenna and to make sure those fifteen years of marriage were not a lie or a waste of time. Daniel decided he would contact the Sergeant Major of the Army. He told the Sergeant Major he would like to make arrangements to have a leave of absence from the army to mend situations back home. Sergeant Major looked at Daniel and thought about it for a few minutes and then decided to grant the leave of absence. Daniel was so grateful for the Major's decision and waited to board the plane with other soldiers who were going home.

On the way back to California, Daniel pondered what he would say to Jenna. It had been years since he had left for Afghanistan. It would be about a twenty-five-hour flight back to California, so Daniel figured he might as well get comfortable and think of what he was going to tell Jenna. He hadn't seen her in so long, and he didn't know what to expect when he saw her. He decided he would just rest, take a nap, and either let his dreams give him an idea of what to do. Daniel also thought about winging it and just letting her know on the spot how he felt and what he wanted out of their relationship. As his mind kept racing, his eyes became heavier and heavier. Soon, he found himself asleep on the plane.

His dream felt so real. He was still in his seat on the plane, but something was wrong. All the soldiers who were on the plane with him were not there. No seat was filled and it was too quiet. Daniel decided to investigate the plane's cabin. Both floors of the plane were empty. Daniel thought that was very odd. He decided to try and gain access to the cockpit, but there was something odd about the cockpit entrance. There was blood oozing from under the door.

As soon as Daniel pulled the door as hard as he could, he was horrified. The pilot and copilot were indeed in the plane, but they were zombies. As soon as Daniel made his way in and realized what happened, the copilot zombie had turned around and let out a groan. That caused chills to go down Daniel's spine and the hairs on the back of his neck stand up. As soon as Daniel turned around, he was faced with all the soldiers and flight attendants as zombies. Daniel was frozen. There was nowhere to go. Soon all the zombies had surrounded him and started to bite him. At that moment, Daniel screamed in pain. One of the zombies shook his arm. Again, it shook his arm.

Then, the zombie started to talk and said, "Staff Sergeant Blaze!" Daniel looked at the zombie confused. How could this zombie talk?

Again, the Zombie shook Daniel and yelled, "STAFF SERGEANT BLAZE, WAKE UP!" At that moment the dream went dark. Daniel opened his eyes to his fellow soldiers surrounding him.

One of the soldiers said, "That must've been one hell of a nightmare, Serge."

"You have no idea," Daniel replied.

"Well now that that's over, you can get the hell off the plane. We landed in LAX about a half hour ago. I think you're the only one left that has family still waiting."

Daniel exited the plane and proceeded to the baggage claim. While waiting for his bags, Daniel heard a woman's voice behind him say, "You bastard! I thought you weren't going to come back home." Daniel simply smirked when he heard this. He remembered that voice. He turned around to meet his wife.

She had not changed much in the seven years he had been away. She was a tall cardinal-red haired woman with hypnotizing crystal-clear blue eyes and a beautifully copper toned body. She was like an angel. He hugged her, and the two shared a tearful and passionate kiss. The two could not believe that that was actually happening. Once they finally were able to collect themselves, they picked up Daniel's bags and headed to the car. Daniel hadn't spoken a word since he got off the plane.

He decided to break the silence and jokingly said, "Jeez baby, you could have warned me that you were coming, I almost thought I was either going to have to stay at the airport overnight or arrange for an Uber to pick me up."

Jenna laughed and said, "You really think that I am going go another minute without seeing you?" Daniel smiled. He didn't want to go another minute without seeing her either.

It was a long drive home. It was weird though because instead of driving to their house in Anaheim, they were headed to Irvine. Daniel was confused and anxious. He decided that he would ask Jenna why they were going to Irvine. All of the sudden, she had a sad and serious face.

"I couldn't stay in that house anymore, not after..." Jenna paused and pulled over to wipe tears from her eyes. Daniel understood then what happened but let Jenna continue. "... So, after that happened, I sold the house and remembered how you and your mom would always talk about moving back to Irvine, the quiet and safe neighborhood. I found a house with three floors. It has an attic and a basement. I took care of all your stuff to make sure it was clean before you came back and messed it up..."

Daniel laughed because he knew he would make himself right at home and make a mess to make sure he knew where everything was. Jenna playfully socked him and continued, "...and there is one final thing you're going to love. There is someone really anxious to meet you." Daniel was confused. Besides going to see his mother who else in town here is excited to see him?

The two finally arrived at the house. Something was strange though. He heard yelping like a tiny dog barking from inside the house. Right after he heard that, his heart beat like it hadn't before. Suddenly and immediately, his confusion turned into excitement. Jenna led Daniel into the house to the room where the source of the barking was coming from. There at their feet behind a baby gate stood a small German Shepherd-Siberian husky puppy. It was as small as a Chihuahua with a lot of fluff. Its coat was all black, except for the white-boot-like paws and middle section of its stomach. The strange trait that Daniel noticed was that one eye was sky blue and the other an emerald-green color.

"His name is Balto. I wanted to keep him a surprise until you got here. Besides, I can tell he already likes his dad because you're the first person to see him that he didn't start barking at."

Daniel walked closer to Balto. The puppy tried to stand up and lean on the fence but was too small to reach the top. Daniel reached in with both hands to pick Balto up. He could not believe that Jenna had done that all for him. It's almost as if all his dreams were coming true.

As it turned out, all his time for his service in the army was what made the dream possible. Because he was a high-ranking officer, it helped pay for the house. Later Jenna admitted that her saying that she wanted to break up with him was all a ploy to get him back to California. She also said she wasn't alone. She had help from the sergeant major, Sev, and Shauniee Stylez himself.

At first Daniel was angry, but then he couldn't help but appreciate what Jenna had done. He even found himself laughing because he figured that he probably would have done the same thing. Jenna's plan was one that took a while to actually formulate. Sergeant Major had received a letter from

Jenna months before she mentioned anything about a divorce to Daniel. She let the Sergeant Major know her situation. First, he had said it would be difficult for leave and that he would try to work something out. After that letter, another followed for Jenna stating Daniel's leave would be allowed once he asked for it.

That was where Jenna's plan hit a rocky take off. Jenna then remembered Daniel's old buddy Sev. She thought of how she would contact him. She decided to just play it by ear. She asked herself how many Sev's would there be in the army? Of course, with her luck, it turned out that he was the only Sev in the army. She asked him to try and convince Daniel to come back home and give him advice about contacting Shauniee Stylez to see what he would say. Of course, the man that stated he was "The Best to Ever Do It" truly lived up to his word. His advice eventually influenced Daniel's decision and convinced him to talk to the Sergeant Major. As Jenna finished explaining her "chain of messages," Daniel became more impressed than he had ever been with Jenna. He didn't think that her plan seemed easy to execute.

Daniel took time out of his day, and while spending quality time with Balto and Jenna, he wrote letters of thanks to Sergeant Major and Sev. Major said that Daniel could come back whenever he wanted, just say the word and he'd be welcomed back on base with an open door and open arms. Sev wrote him back saying "No problem, bro. Just be safe. Don't finish celebrating just yet, because I will be there soon as well to really get the celebration going." Daniel was ecstatic to read that.

Life was coming together. He then remembered Shauniee Stylez's thank you and decided to get on snapchat and personally thank the man himself for the little plan. Shauniee humbly replied to him saying, "Thank you again for your service in the army! I am glad that I was able to help out one of my Manboy Mafia Members." Daniel then thought to himself about it for a second... *That's it!* He'll invite Shauniee over, so that the welcoming home party for him and Sev would be perfect. With Shauniee, Daniel knew that he would take the party to the next level.

The next morning was perfect because it happened to be "Take off Tuesday," which was Shauniee's day off where he would occasionally answer snaps. Of course, Daniel again got the attention of Shauniee at the most opportunistic time, and of course, Shauniee replied right away as if to greet an old friend. Daniel could not keep his excitement in any longer and yelled, "Woohoo!!" That made Balto howl for the first time. The scene made Jenna giggle and record the ordeal to send it to Shauniee to bring more attention to the trio. Both Daniel and Jenna sent a message to Shauniee saying that his dog Stylez was more than welcome to come with him. This made Shauniee happy because he hated leaving Stylez at home. So everything was set. The party was just days away. Sev's flight was coming in that night, and Shauniee's flight was coming the next morning.

Daniel allowed the guys to unpack completely and get comfortable. Stylez and Balto got along very well. Stylez was laid back, and Balto was a little ball of fluff, playfully nipping at Stylez. Days went by, until finally the day of the party had arrived. That was the day when people would get crazy! Sure enough, word got out somehow that Shauniee Stylez was in

California and the people that showed up knew exactly where to go. Over five hundred people ended up at the party!

At first Daniel, Jenna, and Sev were worried everything would go wrong. But, everything went fine... until it struck midnight.

The moon began to change into a burgundy red, and people began fighting each other. Daniel, Shauniee, Sev, and Jenna looked at each other in horror.

"What the hell is going on?" Sev and Daniel wondered. Shauniee and Jenna seemed to know what was going on.

"Follow me," Jenna said hurriedly. The three guys followed Jenna into the basement. Daniel had not checked out the basement. It was almost like a tunnel-like cave that went on for miles. They came to a door that had a huge sticker with "Die Epic" (Shauniee smirked and shook his head at that.) and a thumbprint scanner that only opened with Jenna or Daniel's. When Jenna opened the door, there were weapons, armor, and vehicles of various kinds. Daniel and Sev were impressed. They saw some shit in the army, but that took the cake. When the four gathered their weapons, they went back up to the chaos ensuing the house and neighborhood. They all looked to Shauniee, and he was startled for a second and said, "If we're going to die, it might as well be epic!"

They fought to the death, yet the violent crowds kept coming! They decided to attempt to use one of the vehicles that resembled the X-Jet from X-Men, in the basement and flew it up to the moon to see what was going on. An evil dictator by the name of Ryan Pain had a machine that caused the moon to turn red make people on earth angry and violent all the time. Shauniee and Jenna attempted to distract Pain with success.

Daniel and Sev were able to disable the machine. Then, came the difficult task at hand, and that was to take out Pain. They had guns that when they fired upon Pain, he instantly went down. Everyone breathed a sigh of relief. The moon started to turn back to its normal white color. The gang packed up all the machinery, weapons and Pain himself into the jet. They headed home back to earth to see if everything was back to normal.

At first, they were a bit skeptical about whether or not the town was back to normal. As soon as they exited the basement to the backyard of the house, the five hundred people that were at the party were still there as if nothing had happened. One of the party goers even said, "Hey I found them!" Apparently, the party goers weren't aware of the whole situation, but they somehow remembered that the four of them had slipped away for quite some time. The party continued, and one party goer pulled a string and a white neon sign lit up that said, "DIE EPIC." The party went on until the next day. Then, everyone had to go home because the next day was Monday, or in other words, back to work or for those who had the day off "Manboy Monday!" Shauniee told everyone to get home safe. As soon as everyone was gone, it was Daniel, Jenna, Sev, and Shauniee again.

Sev spoke up and said, "Well, that was one hell of a welcome back, Jenna." The guys all looked at Jenna.

"Well, I didn't expect all that to happen," Jenna said smiling.

Sev said, "Well I'm going back to base tomorrow, so Afghanistan will seem like nothing. Thanks again for having me."

"It wouldn't have been a party without you, brother," Daniel said.

Shauniee then spoke up, "Well, guys. It's time for me and Stylez to leave."

Daniel said, "Don't worry, bro. I'll take you and Sev to the airport."

Off the three guys and Stylez went to the airport. Jenna waved goodbye to Sev and Shauniee with Balto in her arms. When the trio arrived at the airport, Daniel unloaded all the bags for Shauniee and Sev. Sev's flight was the first to go, but before he left, he hugged Shauniee who gave him a Die Epic sticker. Daniel gave Sev a medallion with a yin and yang symbol, but instead of circles, it had wolf paws on the inside of both halves. That helped him get through rough times by just repeating, "Everything gets better in the end."

Shauniee's flight to New Jersey was up next. First, Daniel gave Stylez a pat and said, "Be a good boy!"

Then Daniel turned to Shauniee and said, "Thank you for everything you've done man. You are truly the best to ever do it."

Daniel gave Shauniee a hug and in return Shauniee gave Daniel an exclusive Die Epic t-shirt that was in army UCP colors. Daniel said it was the greatest shirt that he'd ever seen. Daniel left Shauniee at the terminal and started driving home.

For the next few years, Jenna and Daniel became closer. Daniel decided he would take a backseat on going back to the army and start his family life again with Jenna. Sev ended up becoming a Sergeant Major. Shauniee ended up getting a lot of media attention from his snapchat that he actually ended up making and staring in his own movie.

About the Author

J.D. Delgado is an author who loves writing stories that tickle the minds of readers. He was born in Orange, CA, but spent most of his life in Anaheim and Fullerton. J.D., as a child, was a great writer and speller. In 2015, he decided to pursue his passion for writing. In 2016, J.D. decided to use his dreams and nightmares as inspiration for his stories. He aspires to be on the list of greatest authors ever known.

The Unexpected

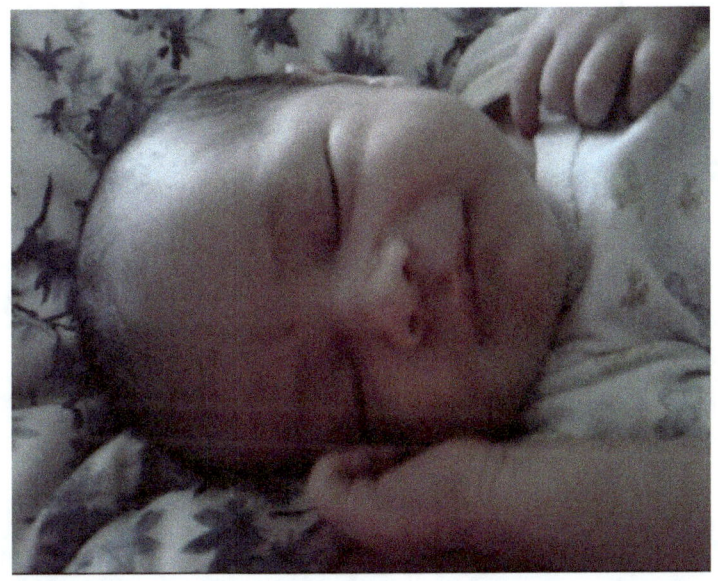

Anna Deutsch

"In three words I can sum up everything I've learned about life: it goes on."

Robert Frost

The week of my twenty-first birthday was when my life changed. I had no idea what I was going to do or what was going to happen next. I had just begun to make a list of priorities for my future. All I knew was my life had changed forever. How could two pink lines impact my life so much? The uncountable days of exhaustion had me amazed. How could one person be so tired all the time?

I would lie down for a nap after work and not wake up until the next morning. I was so sick all the time. My doctor had explained feeling ill and weak was to be expected. I knew quickly this would a challenge like no other I had ever had before. Then, it became difficult to sleep. No position was comfortable, even with several pillows surrounding me. Then, the temperature wouldn't be quite right. Sleep paired with simple daily tasks like dressing or shaving my legs were no longer simple anymore.

To compound matters, my physical appearance was no longer one I recognized. I waddled like a duck in black polka dot pajama pants with a t-shirt stretched over my watermelon belly and sandals on swollen feet. There was a timeline. Yet somehow, my body defied it. I began to feel completely out of control not knowing what would happen when. My life was up in the air, and all I could do was keep going to the doctor and wait. After reasoning, the doctor proceeded with another ultrasound. It was time, and he directed me to come back the following Sunday night. I was overjoyed and overwhelmed. Somehow, knowing I would deliver soon created many fears of the unknown. This would be a huge responsibility; this was someone's life.

I eagerly checked the navy-blue tote that held my preferred items. Those items were to somehow help me through a situation I'd never been through before. The tote included my silver iPod Shuffle with calm music my brother loaded for me, my favorite pillow in a pink-flowered case, to make me feel at home, a silk navy blue robe, to cover all body parts, and a pair of orange, white and pink striped slippers because the hospital floor is cold. Lastly, there was hand sanitizer because hospitals are full of sick people.

I had always imagined the pain would be in my lower abdomen, so I was not prepared when the pain went to my lower back. Kristie, the nurse, popped in to check on me about midnight, encouraging me to rest in between contractions. I thought, *She must've never been in labor before.* I silently pondered how someone could sleep between random stabbing back pains. I requested some ice chips and sent Kristie on her way. I was unable to make myself comfortable in the bed. I decided to start walking around. I had to take the metal IV pole with me.

I stepped out of my room, heading right onto the floor with maroon carpet and wooden handrails throughout, continuing in the oval shape of the ward. It was nearly 3am. The doctor saw me and instructed me to lie down. The Pitocin was lowering my blood pressure to 80/40 and had to be stopped for a while. However, to continue moving forward with the labor, a gel was applied to help my water break. I was no longer allowed to get up from my bed because my water breaking could be a safety hazard. I rolled my eyes. What did other women do when their water broke naturally? Did it turn into a slip and slide? I think not. I could feel myself becoming more irritable and anxious.

Without the Pitocin, I was no longer having contractions. I drifted off to sleep.

The doctor came in around 5am, stating he would turn the Pitocin back on because my heart rate had stabilized at 100/60. The pain was worse that time and more frequent. I finally asked for some pain medicine around 6am, but I couldn't tell the difference with or without. It was as though I asked for pain medication, but the doctor gave me water. At 10am, I asked for an epidural. I honestly didn't imagine the process taking that long. I was exhausted. Then, it was about 12noon. I had barely closed my eyes all night. The pain was intense, and I was forced to stay in bed waiting for the epidural.

Finally, in came the anesthesiologist. The epidural was inserted while I was having a contraction. My eyes widened. I tried to calm myself by chanting, "You can do this. You can do this." The contractions were really bad by then. They were so bad that I didn't feel the needle go into my spine. A catheter was inserted too because I would be temporarily paralyzed from the waist down. Finally, I felt relief from the pain. The doctor came in to pause the Pitocin again because our heart rates were too low. The baby's heart rate monitor band going across my abdomen could no longer read a heartbeat. I was in tears. I had read about babies dying from the distress of labor. All I wanted was a safe, healthy baby. The doctor removed the heart monitoring band and applied a red heart rate monitor stick that suctioned to the baby's head. The baby's heart rate was low. That was due to a combination of the water breaking hours ago and the Pitocin forcing labor. The roller coaster of emotions combined with lack of sleep and exhaustion from the contractions had caused me to reach my limit. I decided to rest.

The doctor continued to come in every couple of hours, checking my dilation. Positive words expressed the progress, "Slowly but surely." I felt at ease, patiently waiting for the arrival. The doctor awakened me around 6pm to explain the baby's heart rate was no longer stable and I had stopped dilating. The birth plan was out the door; the only plan was to keep my baby safe and healthy. I was willing to do anything. The doctor said, "It's time to take the baby out; we need to do a C-section." I immediately said, "Okay." Everything moved quickly. My hospital bed rails were shifted up and wheels unlocked. The staff pushed me into the surgical room for the procedure. A new medicine was pushed through my epidural site to ensure I didn't feel pain. I couldn't see anything.

There was a blue tarp-like cover to shield me from seeing the C-section. I laid there as several doctors and nurses communicated between each other. I started to feel very nauseous with the taste of metal in my mouth and requested something to help before I became sick. Another medicine was pushed through, and I was quickly relieved. At 7pm, I heard the cry, such a sweet cry of uncertainty. My baby was held up briefly for me to see. Tears of joy fell from my eyes. My baby was taken into another room to be cleaned, weighed, and have all the other tasks performed on a newborn. I was presumably sewn up; then, my bed was pushed into a new room.

That room was smaller than the first, though there was still a bed along with a fold-out couch and bathroom. The bathroom did not have a tub or a regular shower. Instead, there was a sink, toilet and a handheld white shower head and hose connected to the wall for showering, with a drain in the floor.

There was an armoire across from the foot of the bed instead of closets near the headboard.

Next to my hospital bed was my baby boy in his bassinet. It was almost like staying in a hotel, with a private room, bathroom and room service. Someone came in every two hours to make sure I was still alive and to remind me it was time to nurse. Most became a blur because of the pain from the C-section and the exhaustion from the labor. Nobody tells you that when breastfeeding, the milk isn't there when you give birth. I was pumping colostrum that the nurse would mix with water for my baby. My baby lost 10% of his weight before we even left the hospital. I did not know how long I would stay at the hospital.

By the fourth day, I was able to walk slowly. There was a special bandage over my hip to hip C-section incision, and I was not allowed to lift more than ten pounds for the first month. Feeling ready to return to the comfort of my home with my baby, I was finally given a clearance. My baby was carried down in his car seat, and I was pushed down in a wheelchair. Reaching the car, I sat in the backseat with the baby and the twenty packages of diapers from the hospital during the ride home.

Who would have thought all of that would come from two pink lines?

About the Author

Born and raised in Colorado. Anna Deutsch is a mother of one boy. She is the oldest of three siblings, with two younger brothers. Anna enjoys music, reading and new experiences. She is currently working on furthering her education, with plans to be more self-sufficient, with hopes to own her own business someday.

My Year

Crystal Dickinson

"It's always hard to deal with injuries mentally, but I like to think about it as a new beginning. I can't change what happened, so the focus needs to go toward healing and coming back stronger than before."

Carl Lloyd

Hepatitis C is a blood transmitted disease that primarily effects a person's liver. The virus, called HCV, was identified in 1989. It can be transmitted through intravenous drug use, poorly sterilized medical equipment, and blood transfusions. I acquired it by blood to blood contact. I was born on a rainy Wednesday afternoon at Fountain Valley Hospital. That was also the day my mom learned she had HCV. My mother's doctor informed her she had Hepatitis C and that, during labor, I had contracted it. She was devastated. They assured her that because I acquired the disease as a baby, my body would build antibodies naturally and I would never have a problem with it. She didn't believe them.

As I was growing up, I always thought it was normal for kids to have blood drawn every few months. I dread going because I hated needles. My mom had to go quite often too. She would always say they were treating her like a lab rat. I asked my mom about it, and she said she was helping try out a new medicine and it could help lots of people. Over time, she started acting differently. She was sleeping more and eating less. She would hardly get out bed. She didn't talk as much. That went on for a year before the treatment was over. The treatment didn't work.

When I was in seventh grade, my mom took me to get a biopsy. Apparently, something in my bloodwork looked off, so they were going to take out a piece of my liver for examination. I thought it was so cool. The nurses and the doctors were funny, and I got to miss school for a few days. My parents were a little worried, but I could not have cared less. The room I was put in had a bed next to a computer and medical machine that beeped when I was hooked up to it. There were two chairs and a screen covering half the room. They put me under for the surgery, and

I woke up almost as soon as they finished putting the bandages on me. I surprised the nurse because I was trying to sit up before I was fully awake. My parents had just left for lunch, so after the nurse left, I was alone with the awful hospital television. The worst part was that I wasn't allowed to eat for a whole four hours after the biopsy. My mom was upset that she wasn't there when I woke up, but I just thought it was funny.

After my biopsy, it became clear to the doctors the virus was active in my liver and that my body had not created antibodies to fight it. My mom cried. We began meeting with doctors regularly after that. My mom wanted to get all the information. She encouraged me to ask any questions that came to mind, but I could almost never come up with any. We met with doctors for about a year. Some doctors said I should take the medicine while I was still young, thinking maybe it would work better. Other doctors said I should wait until I was eighteen because the medicine could do permanent damage to my body while I was young.

My parents were also split. My dad wanted me to take the medication when I was older after what he saw it had done to my mom. My mom believed my best chance for a cure was to do it while the odds were in my favor. Finally, they both decided that it should be up to me if I took the medicine. It was at thirteen years old when I made one of the biggest decisions of my life. We spent a while preparing. My mom was so adamant about wanting me to eat more because the medicine causes weight loss. We only had one doctor at that point. She was a short brunette lady with big glasses who was always smiling and happy, which was weird to me because no one else was really happy with what was going on. She went going over what I should expect while on the medicine. I didn't pay attention much to what she said would happen to me. I remember her assuring me that if the side effects were too severe, they would immediately stop the treatment. She also told me they often did that when kids took it. When I heard that, I started getting more nervous.

My dad was upset with my decision, but he never tried to stop me. I really like that although he disagreed, he never stopped supporting me. It didn't stop him from looking so disappointed though. My last doctor visit before starting the medicine was at the hospital where I got my biopsy. The room was meant for kids and had a dry erase board for kids to draw on. It was my last chance to back out. I remember it was the only time my doctor wasn't happy-go-lucky. She asked me, not my mom, if I was sure that I wanted to do it. At that point, my mom was even nervous. She had been so strong and confident up to that point, so it was jarring to see her look so uncertain. She confessed to me she wasn't sure she wanted me to go through with it. My doctor told me there was a chance the treatment wasn't going to work. I could potentially go through what my mom did for nothing. I said I was ready.

There were two parts of the medicine I had to take: two pills of Ribavirin at breakfast and dinner and a shot of Interferon I had to inject in places with a lot of fat once a week. The shots they gave me were different than the ones given to my mom. They came in white boxes of four and looked like white tubes with two blue ends. I was scared of the shots and had my mom do them for me.

In the beginning, I didn't feel any different. I was still my happy, excited self. But slowly, things changed. Food started smelling weird. The smell of chicken made me so nauseous I had to leave the room. I felt a little sluggish, but nothing serious. When I started high school, I was fine. I was a little bit more reserved, but fine. I made a few friends and had fun. Then, we moved. I wanted to make friends at the new school, but it was hard. I couldn't build up the energy to talk to people. When I managed to talk to someone, I just couldn't enjoy it. Things felt so difficult, and I felt so isolated. I stopped being happy. I kept a little black journal where I wrote about my feelings. I wrote about how everything made me angry and about how I just wished I could feel better. I can't look at that journal now without crying.

I talked to my mom about taking classes online. She agreed, and the next day, I signed out of my high school. I was returning my books when I couldn't find the library. I was lost, my arms hurt from the books, and I couldn't handle it; I felt entirely overwhelmed. I sat down on a short brick wall, and I cried. I called my mom, and she came and took care of everything. I knew I was different from before, but I couldn't tell if it was the medicine or puberty. I thought that maybe that was the way I would be.

My first year of high school felt absolutely awful. Online school helped with my anger. While I wasn't angry anymore, I still wasn't doing great. I couldn't eat; nothing felt fun to me; I didn't talk to anyone. I was alone almost all the time. I was depressed. When I finished the medicine, the world looked different. It was brighter out, and I didn't feel tired. I felt good again. My doctor was so happy I managed to finish the treatment. She told me I wouldn't know for another three months if I was cured. My mom was so glad I was off the medicine. I had to go in for bloodwork once a month, but at that point, I was used to needles.

As the three-month marker drew closer, my mom, dad, and I grew more and more nervous. At my final bloodwork, my mom was super anxious. She didn't want my year to be a waste. Even when it was over, we wouldn't know. We would have to wait for another meeting with my doctor. When my appointment came, we had to wait in a sterile, white room with only one chair. My doctor came in super excited to tell me I was cured. My mom cried.

Today, I am doing much better. Life isn't always perfect, but I am no longer in the state I was then. Looking back, I am so glad my parents let me make that choice. While it was, without a doubt, the worst year of my life, I was able to become healthy. I also learned so much about some awful emotions. I learned I never want to feel hateful, angry, sad, and alone. I try every day to stay positive, even when it's hard. I've already been at my worst, and I know the only way to go is up.

About the Author

Crystal Dickinson is currently a student at Crafton Hills College and was an actress in the movie Distortion Social Media Story. She was very excited to make her debut into writing with "My Year." She is a loving cat mom and a great daughter.

LIFE'S

Rayford J. Elliott

"Rejoicing in hope; patient in tribulation;

continuing instant in prayer."

Romans 12:12

It is common for most of us to run into a railroad crossing. Any railroad track that runs across a street is a railroad crossing. It is quite common while driving on a street for a train to be coming. Usually, before the train gets to the street, the red lights begin to flash, and the rail arm proceeds to come down to its horizontal position across the street. When that happens, there is no way you can cross the tracks. So, what do you do?

This is what I have encountered many times on my way home after work. I commute every day. Sometimes, the freeway gets so crowded. So, I take a shortcut to bypass some of the heavy traffic. However, I always run across the railroad crossing on the side street. Sometimes, I do not beat the train that is crossing. I can hear the train sounding its horn from far away. Each time, I speed up to try and beat the train before the rail arm comes down to block me from crossing. Depending on how far I am away, sometimes I make it through. Other times, it catches me, and I am stuck until the train passes by.

At this crossing, the trains that pass by carry a heavy, long load of boxcars, sometimes one or two miles long. So, you can imagine how long the wait would be. I have waited up to thirty-five minutes. That was a train carrying two or three miles of cargo attached to it.

The most interesting about this situation is there is nothing I or anybody can do about. I can only wait until the train passes or if possible, I can turn around and take the busy freeway route which was my first intention to avoid in the first place. Unfortunately, I have tried that but to no avail. As I turn around to go take the freeway route, I found that it would take me longer to get back on the freeway. So, in those two instances, I turned around and went back to wait for the train to pass.

There is a lesson I learned from this experience that is applicable to life itself. First, in that situation, there was not anything I could do about the blockage in the pathway, but I could see the end coming, and it was just a matter of moments that the obstacle would be removed from my pathway. What was needed in that situation was patience. When I turned around and gave up, my waiting time ended up being longer; I turned back not, knowing the route I was trying to avoid took more time. Thus, instead of it taking me thirty-five minutes to cross, it took me about an hour and a half. As I returned, I could not retrieve my old position in the line of waiting cars because other cars had filled the line, and I ended up much further behind.

What are some of life's railroad crossings that we may encounter? In life, we may experience the crossing of a broken home, a broken marriage joblessness, health problems, kids running wild, debt that has put you in quicksand- seem like you are sinking more and more in debt, sleepless nights because there is no peace of mind, worry, drugs or alcohol addiction that you just don't seem to be able to break away from, sexual addiction, and oppression and abuse by the system. All these things can keep you at a standstill in life, but you can overcome them. Sometimes, they may seem tantamount, and you just don't see a way to exit. Sometimes, you may go forward then go backward or in another direction, but yet and still, you are in the same situation. What do you do?

The way to deal with life's railroad crossings is to make sure God is in the mix because He will give you wisdom and understanding to bring you out of these obstacles. Sometimes, you try on your own, but it is to no avail. Seek God's help. He will make a way.

God is the key to overcoming your life's railroad crossing. There is a scripture that you can use to help you through these ordeals. Romans 12:12 tells us *"Rejoicing in hope; patient in tribulation; continuing instant in prayer."* God provides for you a way to deal with these life's railroad crossings. When I ran into the railroad crossing on my way home from work, my patience was too short. I did not wait. Instead, I attempted another route which resulted in taking more time. I did not apply the wisdom and understanding God has gifted me with.

During the times you face a railroad crossing, be sure to **keep your hopes high, be patient in times of trouble, and learn to pray instantly**. As far as prayer is concerned, sometimes we wait until our appointed time to pray, but there are times we can use the weapon of prayer when it is necessary for the situation at hand. Prayer not should only be used instantly, but continually.

When you are at life's railroad crossing, reach out to Jesus. He will put a river in your desert. He will put a road in your wilderness. Reach out to Jesus. With Jesus, when you are pressed, you will not be crushed. When you are perplexed, you will not be despair. When you are persecuted, you will not be destroyed. When you are down, you will not be defeated. You can overcome your life's Railroad Crossing.

About the Author

Minister Rayford Jones Elliott is a minister of the gospel of Jesus Christ. He is a devout follower of Christ Jesus because he loves the Lord with his whole heart. As a minister, he teaches and preaches the Word with great fervency in an attempt to save the lost by bringing them into the knowledge of the truth. In his local church, where he has been a member for over fifteen years, Minister Elliott serves as the president of the Men's Fellowship. He conducts weekly discussion groups, thereby demonstrating his dedication to the spiritual development of men. It is his desire to instill in them the same love and zeal for Christ Jesus that he possesses.

The Happiest Place on Earth

Caroline Ferrer

"So many tangles in life are ultimately hopeless that we have no other appropriate sword other than laughter."

Gordon W. Allport

1993 was a time for Disney magic. We were in the middle of Disney's golden era of animation. Every cool kid had the Disney backpacks with matching lunch pails. I heard popular girls talking about their family vacations to Disneyland. I had never been to Disneyland; so, hearing those extremely lucky fourth graders talk about an experience so magical, I couldn't help but feel envious and shame. I was embarrassed that my parents were too poor to take my siblings and me on such an extravagant family trip, and I was ashamed of their pending divorce.

On a beautiful cool spring morning, I overheard my mother on the phone with my uncle, asking if my older sisters could go with his family to Disneyland that day. I saw my chance to be one of the cool kids. I knew I had to act quickly. I immediately asked if I could tag along. I promised I wouldn't bother anyone or be in the way. My mother told me she wasn't sure if there was room for me, but she said to get ready just in case. When my aunt and uncle showed up, what felt like hours later, I quickly jumped up and asked if I could go. My aunt, without hesitation, said, "No." They did not have a seat for me. She proceeded to walk back to her van. I realized then she did not really want my sisters to go, let alone me.

My heart sank, and I felt the tears welling up. I tried my hardest not to cry in front of everyone. I did not want them to have another reason to ridicule me. I could feel the punch in my stomach and a lump in my throat, as I sulked to my bed. With my face planted into my pillow, I let the tears flow. I knew my only chance to feel that real Disney magic was now out of reach.

My uncle and mother walked into the room I shared with my sisters. My mother called my name several times. I was visibly upset with her. She gave me the hope that my aunt and uncle would let me tag along. When I could no longer ignore her, she apologized, wiped my tears, and held me. My uncle must've felt awful for his wife's blunt response. He told me to dry my tears and grab my sweater. I didn't believe him at first.

When it finally dawned on me that I was going to Disneyland, I jumped up and screamed. I couldn't believe it. I was finally going to Disneyland and couldn't be happier. I wasn't really surprised when I jumped into my aunt's van and saw there was an empty back row. Nonetheless, I was grateful to feel included. I wasn't going to let an uncomfortable car ride ruin the day.

The drive there was quiet and uneventful. I stared out the window the whole time, daydreaming about the magical day. Which ride was I going on first? Will I get to see or possibly meet Mickey Mouse? I could hardly contain myself. It was only when we reached the parking lot when I realized I had forgotten to use the restroom before we left home. In my excitement, I simply forgot to go. Being that a majority of the group seemed to be annoyed with my supposed undeserving invitation, I was too afraid to say I should use the restroom. I didn't want to impose further. Rather than speaking up, I decided to hold it. After all, I didn't have to go in that moment. But, I didn't anticipant just how long the wait was for most rides there.

By the time we were in line for Splash Mountain, I could no longer hold it. I had been in line for over an hour when I tried to leave to use the restroom. My cousin told me I couldn't leave and still reserve my spot in line. He told me he wouldn't save my place either. I was desperately searching for my older sisters or at least my uncle. They must've still been in line for the haunted mansion. My nine-year-old self rationalized staying in line for another hour. I figured, *What's another hour? When will I have another chance to ride Splash Mountain?* So, I attempted to stick it out. Big mistake. I could see the end of the line just around the corner. I was almost there, maybe ten more minutes. The sound of the rushing water was all around me. By that point, I could only walk in small baby steps, much to my older cousins' amusement. I was confident I could make it.

When our roller coaster car pulled up, that was the moment my bladder betrayed me. I could feel warm pee running down my leg. My eyes stayed on the ground. I couldn't make eye contact with anyone. My thought process was if I can't see them, they couldn't see me. The Disney employee instructed me to sit down in the car. When I looked up at him, I could see by the look on his face he was on to me. It was the same face your mother makes when you put the empty milk carton back in the fridge. I continued to keep my head down until we passed faces in line. I felt the faces were staring at me, knowing I had just peed my pants. I held onto the hope that I would become soaked on the ride. With every chance of splashing to hide my embarrassment passing, I knew I'd have to face the music once I got off the ride. Sure enough, the ride was over, and I was completely dry, with the exception of the obvious "I'm nine-years old and peed my pants" mark. Luckily, I had my sweater to hide my shame. I kept it wrapped around my waist the remainder of the day.

My cousins, of course, made their comments about my mishap on Splash Mountain. It took years for them to *almost* forget about it. On the bright side, I no longer had to pee. When it was finally time to leave, my aunt didn't want me to ruin her car with my soaked shorts. She insisted I sit in the cargo of the van, lying on a towel. That was the last time I went anywhere with my aunt. Nonetheless, I felt very fortunate to have been able to go to Disneyland. Now, when we go on a family trip, I sure to make the little ones use the restroom before we hit the road and take plenty of potty breaks.

About the Author

Caroline Ferrer is a student at Crafton Hills College. She plans to apply to nursing school when she completes her Associate Degree in Health Sciences. Her hobbies include baking, exercising, and watching scary movies with her family. She resides in her hometown of Redlands, CA with her husband, two children, and three dogs.

My Trip to Paradise

Juliette Gonzales

"The future belongs to those who believe in the beauty of their dreams"

Eleanor Roosevelt

The most beautiful place I have had the privilege of visiting was Hawaii. During my stay in Hawaii, I was able to experience a once-in-a-lifetime experience. For one week, I was able to engage in various activities, including snorkeling, zip-lining, and water sports. I was engulfed with the beautiful scenery that was Hawaii. I was also able to attend cultural festivities, one of which is known as a luau. Hawaii was filled with wonderment and an unbound captivation of the beauty of Hawaii.

Welina

On the day of our arrival to Hawaii, my mother, who came with me, and I were amazed at the clear blue skies, the dark and light tones of green that encapsulate the entire environment. Hawaii's beauty is simply indescribable, from its natural movement and regality of the ocean to the mesmerizing sight of the forest. We spent the day indulging in the scenery and visiting a vast number of interesting places that Hawaii offers, with the inclusion of witnessing the volcano in all its glory, engaging in playful conversation with the locals. We also got to visit all they different stores Hawaii had to offer. Around each corner, there was always something unique that caught our attention. Within the first day, we were so exasperated with the overwhelming sense of joy that washed over us. That night, I went to sleep knowing that the trip would be one of the best.

Ke Ahi

As my trip continued, my mother and I embraced the new environment that was in completely, by participating in the various activities that were at my beck and call. One activity in particular happened to be the most Hawaiian thing you could find: a Luau. A luau is in essence a bonfire with a feast that includes various forms of entertainment, which were coconut picking, weaving, fishing, and finally the luau dance and cruising on a charter boat. The luau tells a story, mainly through the use of dance. The dances are stylistically different while sharing a very common background and/or story; some of the dances were done with fire. The men and women of the luau were eye drawing and hypnotizing. There was a large feast, that included local food and even a few delicacies. The luau was an exhilarating experience, and I would highly recommend visiting one in the future. This particular Hawaiian tradition involves so many activities loved by all: eating, dancing, drinking, and playing with fire. It was an all-around unforgettable experience, one for the scrapbooks.

Hoike Ai

The next stop consisted of a snorkeling adventure off the coast of Waikiki. Whilst on this adventure, I saw the gorgeous marine life and coral reefs. I was lucky enough to witness all life from sea anemones to large dolphins and even whales. Another once in a lifetime sort of adventure I participated in was Zip Lining through the tall and glorious trees of Waikiki, a complete rush of adrenaline with a slight fear of sudden death made for a great transition out of my comfort zone. After, we hiked down a steep trail. In Waikiki, we came across a huge, breathtaking waterfall; within that moment, I felt I was in complete, utterly at peace. Witnessing that site of God's creation made me realize how beautiful and short this life is. The last noteworthy experience was jet skiing in the vast open ocean again off the coast of Waikiki. Being able to feel the ocean breeze at high speed while looking back at the island is a moment I couldn't possibly forget. All four of these fantastic adventures were made possible by my lovely mother. I was able to enjoy all of these experiences with someone I truly care about. I will forever cherish these memories near and dear to my heart. While we know other adventures await us, I cannot see a place that beats Hawaii.

Aloha

Leaving Waikiki was painful, because it was the trip of a lifetime, filled with laughter and fun. Each day was a new adventure, making endless memories while spending time with my mom. As the days went on, it became bittersweet that we would soon be leaving such a gorgeous place. Hawaii will always have a place in my heart. Perhaps next time, we will spend more time in Honolulu or maybe Maui. There is an extensive amount to see on all seven of Hawaii's islands, and you cannot limit yourself to only seeing one. One piece of advice for those planning a trip to Hawaii is live it up and do not be afraid to try the things that scare you. Hawaii is a breath-taking beauty that all should be required to experience.

About the Author

Juliette Gonzales is currently a student at Crafton Hills College, striving to study in the medical field. Juliette is known for her "creative writing" and is also referred to as a "passionate writer," but she is mainly known for her passion towards medicine. Juliette wants to continue writing as a hobby and keep sharing her stories with others. Her short story "A Trip to Paradise" is Juliette's first published short story.

One Day, I SURVIVED

Crystal Green

"And so it goes, I never meant to hurt you; couldn't stay, but I never meant to desert you; whole lot of things I had to work through; time to heal and restore my self-worth too; confrontation of my fears and anxiety; cried a whole lot of years; I suffered quietly....."

MARSHA AMBROSIUS

One day of my life is happy.

One day, I am mad,

One day, I figure, I'll wake up to something I never had.

One day, I'm dealing with what I love, and one day, I'm not;

One day, I found out love took everything I got.

One day was short and sweet,

One day, all day I spent on my feet.

One day never prepared me for whom I would meet.

One day, I became a woman, responsible with goals to achieve.

One day, too soon, I made up my mind to pack up and leave.

One day in January, I fell so deep in love.

One day, she said, "I love you mommy", thank God in heaven above.

One day, I'd truly learn to be so gentle and so kind.

One day, if I wasn't going to be first, I would surely be left behind.

One day, I made a choice in life to share with all my heart.

One day, he put his hands on me and tore my world apart.

One day, a Tuesday in October, my heart skipped another beat.

One day, I'd be closer to being a queen, and the throne would be my seat.

One day, three months later, he would fight me until I had to flee.

One day, I'd fall down on my knees; "Bring my baby back to me!"

One day, I became a victim of domestic violence and abuse.

One day, I'd feel like life wasn't worth living. So, tell me, what's the use?

One day, oh, that day, I got away.

One day, some day, he surely had to pay.

One day, I'd tell someone that I really needed help.

One day, I took a stand to really help myself.

One day away, safe and sound.

One day was the day that turned my life around.

One day, at dinner with the family, the fight ensued with pistols.

One day, that same day after gunshots rang, he came out from his hiding place asking, "Where's Crystal?"

One day, that day, I realized he abandoned me and our unborn child.

One day, I needed to separate from that male "bitch" for a while.

One day in November, I couldn't wait to be done.

One day, the fourth day, I gave birth to my only son.

One day, I'd wake up loving someone who became my enemy.

One day, I'd had enough of him wanting to beat on me.

One day, I began to fight, for my children and their safety.

One day, I came home from work to find my daughter beat in the face; she looked just like me.

One day, after day, I would suffer through it daily.

One day, I couldn't remember what happened yesterday.

One day, I'd wake up to strangers and no place to stay.

One day began and ended in darkness and despair.

One day, after day, I would feel like less and didn't care.

One day came and went without me knowing how I made it.

One day, all day, to numb the pain, I decided to stay faded.

One day, after day, I chased a high so tough;

One day came, I realized, I could never get high enough.

One day proved to just be too much, and I didn't think I could make it;

One day, I laid in the middle of traffic, "No More!" I couldn't take it.

One day, all I had fought for could easily be taken.

One day, I saw all it took was the large sums of money making.

One day, that day, I prayed so hard, not to be forsaken.

One day, I'd lose myself completely.

One day, I'd come to understand only "I" could complete me.

One day, while I lay down in the grass, she picked me up; "What's wrong with your ass?"

One day, I just got sick of being sick and tired.

One day, soon after that, I discovered how differently I am wired.

One day, I needed to remember who I was, before I knew who to be.

One day, fifteen years later, I'd finally get to see.

One day, I read a quote from Bishop T.D. Jakes that read: "The first thing to do in deciding what stays in my life and what goes is to determine what nourishes and strengthens me."

One day, still to this day, I remember what he said.

One day a victim, one day to survive.

One day to choose between red or black eyes.

One day, you're asleep, one day you're awake;

One day like today, I choose to advocate.

One day too long, just might be one day too late.

One day, after all these years, I've managed to heal and dry my tears;

One day seemed like a nightmare, and now today, I'm waking up with nothing left to fear.

Today, I want to dedicate this piece to all men, women, and children who have been victimized, or survived domestic violence and abuse. Understand that it is never your fault, and there is no good excuse. Know that you are not alone; there are support systems out there that can help you. Don't be ashamed; abusers have a tendency of really trying to break you. Get out, get safe, never look back, or hesitate.

One day, trying to stay, may just seal your fate.

One day may come to be the day, that day may be too late.

About the Author

In Compton, CA, Crystal grew up in a two-parent home of successful entrepreneurs. Her mother always said, "Whatever you choose to do in life, be the best at it. Do more than what is required." Her father taught by example, how to be skilled for independence, from changing a tire to installing a garage door. Excelling academically and athletically, Crystal won every trophy, award, and ribbon she set out to achieve; she was the star of the family. In high school, just to pass the free time, she wrote fifteen chapters of an untitled book that was the craze and conversation of Moreno Valley High. Soon after, she discover a talent that would award her the title "The #1 Braid Specialist." After losing everything she cared about, including herself, she was blessed with a family of strangers who literally picked her up and brought her back to life. As she regained her self-worth, she regained the power she had all along, and is now pursuing all her dreams- one goal at a time.

Operation Wildflower Rescue

Rhonda Hakim

My mother taught me to feel, to love,
My mother taught me to cry, to laugh.
My mother taught me goodness and beauty,
But fate snatched her away suddenly.
Since she was taken I have no rest.
She was my life's vivifying breath.
"LAST NIGHT"
Last night you were here, you came home to me.
You caressed me, loved me, like in the old days.
It couldn't have been a dream, it felt like reality,
I could hear your voice, see your dear face.
The two of us talked and you told me everything,
How you thought about us there, how you were worrying.
"I ALWAYS KNEW"
I always knew how much I loved you,
That I could never leave you behind.
My body may be a worthless worm,
But my soul from yours will never be torn.
Years were passing and the horrible curse came true.
They locked us millions in cattle cars,
And even to you, so faithful to the Almighty,
The murderers denied immunity.
I couldn't do for you a thing.
Watching you my eyes were weeping.
I wanted to follow you everywhere – even
At the price of my life, I thought then.
But on a horrible night, as our train
Slowed down and stopped in the open plain,
They stole you from me, my only treasure.
And yet, I could continue on further.
When the snow fell, I worried about you only,
You were by my side at every step.
When I got tired, you led me ahead,
You stroked me, you held my hand.
This is how I survived the dreadfully big struggle
And I returned to the old abode.
Since then I always search to find you, to reunite,
I expect you morning, noon, and night.
I always knew how much I loved you.
My soul has never left you, followed you even then.
And down here, lifelessly, I play a farce – I mime,
This world is no longer mine.
by Magdalena Klein

Holly Plants a Seed

When I met Scarlet Gilia, she was not someone who particularly mattered in my world. Scarlet was a citizen of the underworld, a prostitute high on anything but life. Her existence was tumultuous and untamed, and as a civilized woman, it never occurred to me that I should ever attempt to befriend someone like Scarlet. It's not that I was too good or that I didn't care. After all, I am a counselor at Caladium Community College. I have built my career on cultivating the dreams and paths of young minds. It just never occurred to me that I could or should impact the life of this misguided wildflower. Then, one Friday afternoon, as I headed towards home, my eyes winced past the glare of the sun and caught a glimpse of tears stained on the face of a seemingly destitute young woman there on a bus bench.

I thought to mind my own business, but my heart was set on guilting my head, and before I knew it, I had parked my car at the nearby café, and I was walking towards this woman who was sitting at the bus bench. I stood behind in her shadow for a moment observing her presence. Her long brown hair was tussled and dirty, her eyes dulled with hopelessness. She was almost childlike and something inside me said, "This is someone's daughter." I quickly sat down on the bench with plans to say something that would matter. Scarlet sniffled with remarkable determination to compose herself and hide a visibly busted lip.

Our eyes met briefly, as I fumbled for words, "Are you okay? What's your name?" I didn't know what else to ask in that awkward moment.

She ignored me, but after some coaxing, she finally snarled back, "My name is Scarlet if you must know, and yes, I'm perfectly fine, and I really didn't ask you to barge into my business." I gasped in offense and stood up to walk away, but my heart was still in "do-good' mode. Before I knew it, I had invited her to join me for lunch at the Foxglove Café across the street.

At first, our words were few, as we looked over the lunch menu. Once we had placed our order, a bit of small talk ensued.

"Scarlet's a nice name. Is that your real name?" I said.

"Does it matter?" retorted Scarlet. Honestly, at that point, it really didn't matter. We were strangers, and I was imposing myself into her world. I just couldn't help wondering how a young woman like Scarlet made the decision to become a prostitute. I'm certain it was not a lifelong dream, and it couldn't possibly be fulfilling. So why? *How did she come to this place,* I wondered? I began asking her about the circumstances that drove her to these choices.

I asked her if she had family and where she had grown up. As it turned out, she had grown up in a very supportive home but had experienced abuse at the hands of a family friend. Believing it was her fault, she remained silent for a few years while the abuse continued. One day, at the age of eleven, when anger and bravery welled up in her chest, she went to her mother and spoke about the abuse. Thankfully, the abuse was immediately put to an end, but the memories continued to churn with perpetual torment.

I too had been through a similar abuse when I was young. My world could have ended up much like that of Scarlet's if it were not for Janie Marigold, a woman in our neighborhood, who had befriended me when I was a young teenager. She had a similar experience in her childhood, and she was the one person that I could always talk to. In many ways, Janie mentored and taught me how to be the strong woman I am today. As I grew up, I knew I wanted to make a difference in the lives of young people as they made critical decisions about how to obtain their dreams. I wanted to be a real and present force that could help another human being find their calling.

As I looked at the young, broken woman sitting across from me, I imagined her future as bright, so I began speaking life into her world. I also told her about my own experience and how I had long blamed myself for what happened even when others told me I hadn't done anything wrong. I told her it took some time for me to get to a place where I could walk away from the hurt to become the woman I am today.

In my own days at college, I had conducted research for one of my psychology classes that encompassed statistics and facts about teenagers and adults of childhood abuse. I knew from research that many victims, like Scarlet and me, become hostage to the memories. As a result, many young victims of abuse never step into their destined calling. Instead, they seek out perpetual abuse, believing it be their sole worth. Scarlet was indeed a textbook case in her own right. I could only hope that our brief encounter might be the spark that called her out into the light.

Halfway through lunch, a largely-built, angry man tattered with misogynist tattoos, came bursting through the café doors. His words spewed venom at Scarlet, who cowered and began apologizing. I stood up and positioned myself between them. I tried to convince her that she did not have to apologize to him.

As I was speaking to her, the brut took hold of my shoulders and shoved me out of the way, telling me to mind my own business, as he yanked her up by the arm.

"Scarlet! Scarlet!" I cried. "Don't go with him. Come with me. You can come with me." I was frantic and felt helpless to save her. One moment, we were enjoying lunch over a bit of chit chat, and the next moment, she was angrily screaming at me in the middle of the café.

"You don't know my life. You don't know me. You think you can save the world 'miss do-gooder?' Well, you can't. This is my world. This is who I am. Sorry to disappoint you, but you can't really save everyone." I was dumbfounded and silenced with mortal shock at the turn of events, fashioned with that proverbial jaw to the floor look. I sheepishly gathered myself together, paid the bill, and headed for my car.

As I walked through the parking lot, I scanned the streets looking for Scarlet and the thug that had heartlessly whisked her away. My chest was pounding as I got into my car and slumped down into the driver's seat. I shouted and sobbed, pounding my fist to the steering wheel until frustration wore itself out. I then composed myself, tidying up my face, combing my hands through my hair to look as if nothing happened. My hands clumsily put the key into the ignition, and I drove home. Once I had settled in for the night, thoughts filled my head about the young woman Scarlet and about the many victims who succumb to hopelessness.

Over the next few days, Scarlet stayed in my thoughts. I couldn't get her out of my head, so I decided to pay a visit to my dear friend Janie. She was getting older in years but still as beautiful as ever. We talked over a cup of tea about days gone by. I told her how her friendship with me had made a difference in my life, and then, I told her about Scarlet. Janie said she once had been befriended by a woman who also mentored her. Talking to Janie always made things better. I told her if I ran into Scarlet again, I too would offer to mentor her if she would let me. At the end of the evening, Janie and I hugged, and upon leaving, I promised to visit her more often.

Over the days and weeks that flew by, I drove down the street, sat at the bus bench, ate lunch in the Foxglove Café but never caught a glimpse of Scarlet. I kept trying to find her everywhere I went. I prayed for her safety and wondered what had become of her. I held onto the hope that possibly words I had spoken into her life had resonated with her soul, that maybe she finally decided to give life a fighting chance. With no concrete answers, I moved on from that experience, but I took to heart that chance meeting. Every time, I counseled a new college student, I thought of Scarlet and longed for her to walk through those doors. If only she had a reason to dream.

Scarlet's New Beginnings

I'm Scarlet Gilia, but you can call me Scarlet. Holly is the woman who befriended me at the bus bench. When I met Holly, she seemed like a nice woman, but she was one of those "do-good" people. She meant well, but I was sure she was wasting her time. I was a prostitute, and she was clearly a successful woman who had her life all figured out. As far as I was concerned, we had nothing in common. My head just wasn't in the right place. I had never really believed in myself. Truth be told, I never imagined a future beyond those mean streets. When I was thirteen, I began drinking and getting high on street drugs. I had been abused for a time, and the street drugs had a way of dulling the memories. My parents tried to help, but I was determined to self-destruct. One day, I ran away and found myself living at a party house. Eventually, a fellow partier introduced me to a pimp. When Holly and I met, I had already been in the game for about seven years. I wasn't ready to walk away though I appreciated the sentiments.

I was awful sorry about the way I blew up at her. She was awful nice; I must have seemed terribly ungrateful. It's just that when my pimp showed up, things got a little crazy. I didn't want anyone to get hurt, and I didn't want more trouble than I was already in. After I left, I thought about Holly often. She had mentioned she had gone through abuse as well. I wondered how life would have turned out differently if I could have just let go of the past. Maybe, I could have been a career woman or at least lived a nicer life. It's just that, my road had long been paved and looking back this all seemed impossible at the time.

When I ran into Janie, I was running for my life. The pimp had left me at a motel and had come back drunk and abusive as usual. Only that time, it seemed worse. Either that or Holly's words had gotten to me. I just knew I needed to get away quickly; that's when I bolted from the room. I found myself in a nearby shopping center, looking for unlocked cars to hide in.

Janie called out to me, "Excuse me, miss, but are you in some sort of trouble?"

I frantically begged her to hide me. Before I knew it, I was in her car, and we were speeding away from the area. She drove for miles before stopping at a donut shop where we sat and spoke for quite some time. Again, there I was sitting across from another woman who wasted no time in trying to save me from myself. We shared stories of childhood experiences, and I found myself defending my path to a woman who once again had been through a similar childhood but had successfully made her way in life. That time, something in me chose to listen. We had long been chatting when Janie mentioned she never got my name.

"It's Scarlet. My name is Scarlet," I said. I'll never forget that look on her face.

She said, "Scarlet? You're Scarlet, as in Scarlet Gilia?" We laughed a bit, and then, she told me about her friendship with Holly. It was then that I realized that life was about to change for the better. In an unexpected turn, Janie offered to take me in for a brief time to help me get on my feet. I accepted her offer and went home with her that evening. I don't know how she did it, but over the course of a few days, Janie inspired me to make a new life for myself. I agreed to enter a drug rehabilitation facility. Later, I worked towards my GED, and one day, I paid a visit to Janie to thank her for all she had done for me. We talked about the possibility of college, and once again, Janie spoke real dreams into my life.

Janie Marigold Blooms a Mission

I'm Janie, the woman you've heard about throughout this story. When I met Scarlet, she was on the brink of saving herself. It was really all her. At that time, I didn't know how things would turn out, but it was clear to me that Scarlet had a calling that somehow involved me and Holly. As if her calling might also be our calling. I suspected that once Scarlet had cleaned up, she would come back into our lives with a clear head and a fistful of dreams. In hindsight, I probably should have called Holly to tell her who I had run into, but I felt that to help Scarlet, we needed to first let her fly. She needed to find her own strength, and indeed, she did just that.

When she came back, there was a new spark in her eyes. Scarlet was a woman ready to take on the world. I talked to her about going to college and mentioned that Holly was a counselor at Caladium Community College. Scarlet seemed eager to meet Holly again. I called up Holly and invited her to dinner. I mentioned I had invited a lovely young lady to dinner who could use some college advice. Holly agreed to join us that evening, so I busied myself with dinner plans and asked Scarlet to set the table.

When Holly arrived, Scarlet answered the door and said, "Hello, Holly. How are you?"

Holly took a second look and then said, "Scarlet? Is that you, Scarlet? What on earth are you doing here?"

After things settled down, I said to the ladies, "Come, sit down, and let's talk about all of this over dinner." The evening carried on with tears and laughter. Holly and Scarlet both agreed that a psychology degree would be a great path for Scarlet. I said, "You know, it's something the way the three of us have come together."

We realized that evening that the key to each of our paths was the person who inspired us to heal and grow, and together, we decided to create a network of mentors who could reach out to young abuse survivors who just needed someone who understood. Like the old saying goes, "It takes a village." I'd like to think that it takes a few wildflowers to inspire one small seed to bloom into its calling.

About the Author

Rhonda Hakim grew up in Orange County, California. She is a writer, marketing professional, and computer geek, who is working towards starting a non-profit organization called *Operation Wildflower Rescue* with the goal of mentoring victims of child abuse. As an abuse survivor, Rhonda is eager to be at the forefront of making a difference in the lives of many survivors. In her free time, she enjoys roller skating and hiking the many trails in her town.

Surprise! No Green Tea Ice Cream

Jessica Huerta

"What can we gain by sailing to the moon if we are not able to cross the abyss that separates us from ourselves? This is the most important of all voyages of discovery, and without it, all the rest are not only useless, but disastrous."

Thomas Merton

Surprise! It is time I tell you about the day I got pretty hyped to get green tea ice cream from a Chinese buffet and didn't end up going. Well, that is a joke, partially. A week or two after I graduated high school, my mom's side of the family set a date for us to all go have dinner to celebrate. The ones who were supposed to go to the dinner were a small part of my family, but they are the members of my family I am closest to. There are my grandparents, who are my world, and I call them Grandpa and Grandma. Then, there are my mom's sisters, Maira and Eliana. Maira and her husband Will are my godparents, so I call them Nino and Nina. Their kids, which are my cousins, are Jonathan, who is closest to my age, and Kaylee and Joycelyn, who are the youngest in our family, would be there. My aunt Eliana, who I call Tia Elly, has one son, and his name is Adam. He is also pretty close in age to Jonathan and me. Finally, my siblings, my sister Gaby, which is short for Gabriela, and my brother Gerry, which is a nickname for Gerardo, planned to come along as well. That was everyone who was going to be at my dinner.

On the day of my graduation, Nina and Tia Elly told me they couldn't have dinner that day, so they told me not to make any other plans on June 23rd because that day would be only for them and me to celebrate. For every occasion, we would always go to a Chinese restaurant called The Lotus Garden, so I was pretty excited to order some of the Green Tea Pistachio ice cream I would always get. It is served in a long clear fancy cup, and it is a bright green color with pistachios. It was my favorite thing to always get, so every time we talked about going there that was what I would look forward to. Leading up to the dinner, my friends would invite me to do things on that day or other stuff came up, but my family insisted I not cancel the plans I had with them. I even was invited to go to L.A. Pride, which I have always wanted to go, but it was on the same day, and I couldn't do that to my family.

On the day of the dinner, Tia Elly wanted me to come over to her house very early, so I could get ready there. I thought it was really weird because usually she wouldn't do my hair or makeup just for a dinner, but I didn't really question it. That morning I woke up, brushed my teeth and hair and put on a white dress with yellow, blue, and purple flower designs all over it and was open in the back. Tia Elly said she would get me ready, so I didn't do much of anything else besides put my shoes on and head out over there with Gaby. When I got there, she curled my hair and put it up in a ponytail and curled my eyelashes and put mascara on them. Finally, when I was done getting ready, she told me everyone was going to meet up at Nina's house for pictures before we went to eat.

As soon as we got to Nina's house, they told me we had to walk in through the side of the house because something was wrong with the front door. My family went in first, and as I walked through the gates of the side entrance, I was looking down at my purse to organize everything. I suddenly look up to see a bunch of people standing up. They screamed, "Surprise." Suddenly, my heart started to race and my skin began to boil. I froze because of how surprised and nervous I was. I was very confused and had no idea how to react because I am not very good with social interaction. Finally, when I had calmed down a bit, I went to say hello to everyone who came to see me and pretended like I just did not have the scare of my life right then.

Once I went back and was able to talk to Nina and Tia Elly, I made a joke saying, "So, I guess I'm not getting that ice cream now." They just laughed and asked if I liked the surprise. The decorations were pretty nice. The walls were covered in streamers, and my name was in bold letters all around saying "Congratulations" and "Class of 2018." Throughout the party, I switched around just hanging out with Jonathan or my grandparents. It was held at Jonathan's house, so he stayed inside whenever he got the chance, but because it was my party, I was not allowed to go inside. I had to socialize with everyone who came all the way from L.A. to see me. Don't get me wrong. It was very nice, and I was so grateful. I just am not a social person.

The party was a very nice gathering, and everyone got a chance to catch up, especially because the part of my family that lives in San Bernardino only sees the people who came every few months. I had to take so many pictures that day that I think I perfected my fake smile for pictures. When I went home, I had a framed photo of my myself from graduation with signatures all around it from the party. My dad saw it and didn't even question it. When my mom got home from her trip, I told her about the party and how I got many nice things, and she seemed to be happy for me. The only bad thing about the whole day was that my brother decided not to go, but I still brought him candy and food from the party. So, instead of my Green Tea Pistachio ice cream, I got many pictures, good memories with my mom's side of the family, and ate homemade food. Also, I got a bunch of money and cool gifts, so I say it was worth it.

About the Author

Jessica Huerta is a first-year college student who was born in Hawthorne, California, in January of 2000. Jessica has lived most of her life in San Bernardino with her two siblings and other family members. Currently, she attends Crafton Hills College as a first-generation college student. She is an eighteen-year-old who enjoys being with her friends, family and pets. She dreams of helping the community and by doing so she will be getting a degree in Sociology, so she can help other people. In her free time, she volunteers or spends time with those dear to her. She was the Vice President at her old school's Key club for two years and completed over 100 community service hours within her four years in high school. She was also a part of her school's varsity swim team. Within just the next few years, she wishes to accomplish so much more.

Yucaipa - L.A. - XO

Fahlicity Leary

"And being so young and dipped in folly, I fell in love with melancholy."

Edgar Allen Poe

It was a beautiful spring morning; the birds were singing as I awoke. I instantly grabbed my phone and began to play The Weeknd, also known as Abel. He has been my favorite artist for four years or so. He records a type of alternative R&B music. I was in such a good mood; it resulted in me singing and dancing as I began to get ready for my class. I was attending Crafton Hills College. It was my second semester of college. After a good hour of getting dressed, I was ready to head to school. Each day, I always stopped by my best friend Tally's house; we would carpool from her house to the school, mainly because only one of us had a parking pass. As we were walking into class, I received a notice that our class was cancelled. So, Tally and I went to get breakfast. During breakfast, we decided to take a trip to L.A.- that day!

Our drive to L.A. was two hours with traffic. Cars were bumper to bumper, the buildings were reaching to the sky, and the clouds were gloomy above the buildings. However, with our excitement, the time flew by! The next thing we knew, we are looking for parking! As we walked up to the Hollywood strip, it was beyond crowded. We had to squeeze around people just to walk through the strip. We could not figure out what to do first. Eventually, we decided to take a Hollywood Tour. Our first stop was the gas station; our bus was on empty. Shortly after, we rolled through Beverly Hills and down Rodeo Drive. Rodeo Drive was so beautiful; the lights and shops had white lights and reminded me of Christmas. On Rodeo Drive, we saw Gucci, Chanel, Versace, and so many other shops we could not afford to shop in. We got to see the homes of famous people; we even drove past Donald Trump's California home. Overall, that tour was filled with interesting stops.

After the tour, we got off the bus, and we were walking down the strip. Then, instantly, a lady dressed in office clothing with glasses pushed me and Tally into a room. We ended up watching a movie, in a theater with just the two of us. The theater was small and had only twelve seats. The movie was called "Dianetics," and Tally yelled "Diabetics? Huh? That's me." We laughed through most of the film, but overall the movie was motivational for the two of us in our state in life. Then, I was talked into buying a fifty-dollar book that I have not yet read.

After the film, we went to three museums. The first one we were not sure what it was to be honest; it was very interactive though! The second was the World Record Museum. I am not going to lie. We got lost! There were so many doors in that museum that we could not find our way out! It took us a while. The final museum was the Wax Museum; we saved the best for last. We went in there looking for Kylie Jenner's wax figure; however, apparently it is not there. We walked into the part with all the "bad guys" (Hellboy, Frankenstein, Hannibal Lecter, and Freddie Krueger). They were all down a dark hallway. The only light was the green or dimmed white light above the wax figures.

At the end of the hallway, there was a door swinging open and closed with loud screeching zombie noises. We could not make it all the way down the hallway. We tried multiple times but kept running out screaming and laughing. We continued through the museum, working up an appetite! We left the museum searching for a hot dog cart. We found one and ordered L.A. hot dogs; they were the main reason we went to L.A. Our hot dog was wrapped in bacon with mayo and mustard on grilled buns! We were beyond excited to eat them! We found a spot, in front of some workers who were taking down a red carpet. We asked someone what was going on. The guy said, "The premiere of the new Marvel film was on the strip!" I went on my Instgram. I thought, *The Weeknd loves Marvel. Let's see if he came.* I checked his story. It said, "2 hours ago," and he had posted himself with the Marvel <u>pass</u>!

I started getting upset because I was two hours too late! Tally and I started talking about The Weeknd (A.K.A. Abel). Then, Tally bit into her hot dog, and I hear a muffled cry for my name. I looked over at her. Her face was stuck following someone, so I looked. I could not believe my eyes. I saw the "199X" jacket that is his merch! Not to mention the XO on it! XO is his label! We got up unsure if it was The Weeknd. We began to follow him at a distance; we did not know how to get his attention. We felt he knew we were following him; he kept slowing down and glancing back at us. We did not want to cause a crowd. People were already looking around thinking there was a celebrity, so we backed off a bit.

Then, he turned into an alley. We followed and watched him walk to his black 2018 luxury Cadillac. He was just about to close the car door, but then we both screamed, "ABEL!" He stopped and looked at us, and we yelled, "Can we get a photo?" He gestured for us to come over! We ran so fast! I personally was not sure what to do, so I hugged him! He was so adorable! He seemed content that we stopped him! I got a video with him! My best friend got a photo with him! And, he had a conversation with us! He asked us, "Did you girls watch the Marvel movie?"

I was a complete spazz; I could not even speak, so Tally responded, "No, we are broke." He said, "It was good; you guys should watch it!" It was a moment filled with adrenaline! We said our goodbyes, and he stated, "Nice meeting you girls." As we were walking away, I looked in my hand, and I was holding that big hotdog with one bite taken out of it! Tally took the hot dog out my hand and threw it in the trash! We walked back to Tally's car. We could not believe we had just met Abel, The Weeknd! I called my mom and dad to tell them. Then, we finally got to the car. We watched the city as we drove off content.

Shortly after getting on the freeway, we couldn't control our excitement any longer. We freaked out like crazed fan girls. On the drive home from L.A., we were shook! In silence, we listened to The Weeknd's music. It was a day for the books.

About the Author

Fahlicity Leary was born the middle child to her father and the oldest child to her mother. She grew up with six younger siblings and two older siblings. This made Fahlicity a strong and determined leader but also a caring and sensitive woman. She spent her younger years in the Coachella Valley and finished her high school years strong in Yucaipa. Early on in her life, her loved ones could see, very clearly, that helping others would be the most fulfilling and rewarding experience for Fahlicity. She always goes above and beyond to please others, even if it means putting their feelings over her own. With a heart of gold and a spirit of ocean waves, Fahlicity has always accomplished everything she put her mind to.

A Day at Disney

Thalia Machuca

"Life itself is the ultimate, unreliable narrator."

Abby

Disneyland is everyone's happiest place to visit, especially for my best friend Ariana. But for me, not so much. It is too crowded and way overpriced.

One day, my best friend kept begging me to go with her, so I finally agreed to take her for her birthday. We got up early the morning of her birthday. It was super cold because not only was it early December, but there was no sun up at all at that time. We put on our most comfortable clothing and made our way to the happiest place on earth. Ariana kept on expressing her joy for Disney the entire ride there, but I was annoyed with the traffic as I was the one driving. The only thing I was super excited for was my favorite ride there: Indiana Jones. After our trip to Disney together, I knew I would have a good story to tell about my all-time favorite attraction at Disneyland.

After the two hours in traffic and bumping, I felt like my head was going to explode. I thanked God I had brought my Naproxen pills with me. Otherwise, it would have been a terrible day. I quickly downed the pills with a bottle of cool water, and instantly, my head felt ten times better. Finally, we rolled up to the entrance, and I could see it on Ariana's face: She had left her eighteen-year-old self at home and brought her seven-year-old self with her instead.

She immediately ran to the ticket booth, so I could purchase my day pass. I purchased my ticket and we went over to the security section to get checked and be let into the park. The first thing I did was run for the bathroom. I had just chugged a bottle of water, so I was feeling a little heavy. The first thing Ariana wanted to do was take pictures of ourselves and post them on her social media. Then, it was time to get on as many rides as we could!

The first one we went to was Space Mountain, another one of my favorites. The line for Space Mountain was only five minutes long because the park had just opened. Right after that one, we went onto Big Thunder Mountain. On our way there, we saw an old lady talking to a bird that was trying to pick up her crumbs. It was definitely a little weird to see, but it was Disneyland. You literally see everything there from proposals to well, old ladies speaking to random animals. Sounds a lot like Snow White.

It was then time for my favorite ride of all time: Indiana Jones. The line was already super long, and it was not even an hour since the park had opened. We waited about forty-five minutes to board the ride. It started to get very hot, and the inside line started feeling humid. While waiting, I kept messing with Ariana because she is genuinely so terrified of that ride. The worker for the ride permitted us to go into the FastPass line because she had seen Ariana's birthday pin. The closer we got to the ride, the more terror I could see on my best friend's face. I mean, I'm terrified of all those rides too, but I still go on them. I was there for a good time <u>not a long time</u>.

It was finally time for us to be loaded onto the jeep-looking cars for the ride. We were waiting at the gate, and as soon as those gates flung open, I was the first one in the cart and ready to go. The ride worker checked all of our seatbelts to make sure they were on, so we wouldn't fly off the ride. We were sent off into the darkness of the ride. I was getting whiplash, and my hair was going everywhere. My voice would probably be gone after the ride, and I was not even mad about it. I felt so happy, like nothing could ruin the moment until... I heard Ariana start screaming in genuine horror. She yelled in my ear that her bag had fallen off the ride. Inside that bag were my car keys, our wallets, ID's, money, etc. My mood was ruined, and I could no longer enjoy the ride. I knew I had to come up with a plan to get that bag back asap.

We got off the ride, and I approached the person who was controlling the ride. I told her what had happened, and she told me we had to wait until midnight when they go through the rides to grab any dropped items. We could not wait that long because one, we both had a speech to present the next morning at 7am, and two, we would have nowhere to go because the park closed at 6pm that day for "Mickey's Halloween Party." On top of all that, we would have absolutely no money to stay hydrated or buy food. I immediately came up with a lie and said that my insulin was in that bag. They would have no other option but to, of course, shut down the ride to retrieve the bag. Now, if I were telling the truth and they refused, I could have sued them, and they knew that, so they shut down the ride, got everyone off and sent about ten cast members to look inside the ride. All I remember was being looked at very angrily by a lot of people, but I did not even care at all. I was unfazed. My friend was worried that they would ask to see the insulin and they would know I lied. I knew they wouldn't because that is personal confidentiality and exposing me in front of everyone like that would only give me a bigger reason to sue them. Again, *if* I were telling the truth.

One of the cast members finally brought out the pink backpack. I grabbed it, strongly apologized, thanked everyone, and quickly made my way toward the exit with Ariana. We were extremely relieved, happy, and very much hungry. We ate a hot dog with macaroni and cheese, topped with bacon bits and just relaxed for a bit. We both promised ourselves to be smarter about securing our belongings next time and also made sure that would not kill our vibe of having a good time. Both of us knew the event would be a good story to tell people someday. So yes, my friend and I did shut down the entire Indiana Jones ride at Disneyland. No regrets.

About the Author

Thalia Machuca is a second-year college student, majoring in health sciences. She hopes to become an oncology pediatric nurse practitioner once she is done with her studies. She lives with her mom and older brother in Yucaipa, CA. Thalia states she looks up to both very much. Thalia has a great amount of love for dogs; she has one mini poodle that is all black with a cute white beard named Roxy whom she treats like a daughter. She enjoys making new friends with her very outgoing personality. Friends often come to Thalia when they have a problem, as she is a helpful person. Thalia's interests include music, mathematics, make-up, shopping and anything else that keeps her busy because she is a workaholic. Thalia is a very determined individual who will not let anything stop her from reaching her goals. She desires to make her family proud and live a happy, successful life.

THE WEAK ARE THE STRONGEST

ISISS PROBY

Weakness

The old beaconed houses held secrets
It kept me up, left me sleepless
The grey sky knows my weakness
My mental thesis

• Su

CHAPTER 1: The Village's Sacrifices

Throughout the entirety of the village, there were many different clans that always migrated. Some ruled, and some eventually faded away to extinction or were conquered by other clans. Some clans and their armies were undefeated; others were just considered weaklings; some were too desperate for power, which made them reckless. Overall, in the near future, these armies and their clans will be conquered. Although the rulers of each clan may not show it, all of them fear and day by day become paranoid for this day to come. In the ancient scroll, when all the clans were united in this year, there were extraordinary baby boys and girls, and they were destined to overthrow each and every ruler.

But, what the ancient scroll did not see was there was a ruler in the shadows, waiting for this day to happen. On this night, all of the mothers, in different villages, miraculously bore children at the same time. The mothers were exhausted and flushed, while the fathers admired or despised the special gift they had brought into the world.

One family, belonging to the Shadows and Winds clan, bore three children, all born on the same day, but there was one that was clearly more developed than the other two. They were born with different hair color, and it was apparent they would have different abilities. Once the babies were born, the unknown ruler sent ninjas to take the babies, but the parents were allowed to give their children items for the babies to cherish and keep. However, they never knew when their child would actually come back home to them.

The mother of the three children handed the ninjas identical necklaces and a picture, while the father planted his quivering lips on each of their foreheads. The mother cried as she held her babies for the last time, while the father only shed a single tear, trying his best to be strong while witnessing the greatest sorrow.

The three gurgling babies were carried away by the unknown men, and they were taken to the underground academy. The academy was hidden from the naked eye; no one could see it unless the ruler allowed them to or they were chosen as well as their family members. No one realized an uprising ruler was taking unordinary babies from different clans to create a powerful army. Then, a family belonging to the Mystical Water Clan bore a baby boy. The father and mother smiled in happiness, but in only a few minutes, their happiness was taken away by the unknown men. The father fought the ninjas, but they were too skilled and unmerciful. They killed the father. The mother's eyes widened with shock, and she wanted to sob, but she had to act strong. The ninjas had to make a decision either to kill her or just to leave, but they decided to leave her to grieve and mourn.

But before they left, she said, "Please let me give something to my baby boy." Although she may have been exhausted but could not let them know, she gave the baby boy a peck and key connected to a beaded bracelet. She tried to touch him for the last time, but the ninja snatched him away from her. As she continued to be heartbroken, she went to her fallen husband

and wept. The ninjas evilly smirked at her and walked out off with her son.

Next, in another village, in the Earth and Rain clan, the newborn baby was destined to be an heir to the throne of the small but strong clan but was taken away by the ninjas. The father of the baby boy despised his son's existence because he wanted to be in power. The mother seemed to be the only one who cared for his wellbeing. The father was willing to give him away, while the mother protested, but no one listened to her.

The ninjas took the child and did not ask the mother if she wanted to send him off with anything. The father did not want the baby boy to know he was an heir, so that there be no traces of the village to be seen or heard of. The father also told the guards to make sure the baby boy had no knowledge of his home village at all. His pride and his jealousy led to that horrible decision, and he did not want to give up his throne. At that moment, the mother began to lose her love for her husband and the respect she had from him.

None of the families knew what was going on with their kids until fifteen years later. The academy had sent each family a picture of their child to give them a sense of comfort and closure. Fifteen years later, the stolen children were doing a strenuous obstacle course, and no one questioned why. Each of the teens were exhausted, but they were driven and kept going because they knew if they didn't there would be punishment and dire circumstances for not completing the task. All of sudden, one of them finally wondered why they were there and how they got there. I wondered a lot of things but did not dare to speak up, even though I knew of my mother and father.

I was the oldest of the triplets because I was born first with purple hair, and now that I am a teen, my hair went from thin, short and straight to very spiky that was past my shoulder blades. All of a sudden, I heard, "Mizuki, focus," my sensei yelled, and I continued the course. After our obstacle course, we ate lunch for brief period of time.

Today, I decided to emerge in the moment as I looked around and noticed there were many kids in this academy. I was interrupted by my sisters who were sitting next to me at a table, asking me if we were able to see Mom and Dad again. I only shut down their curiosity and optimism with the realization that the only chance we had was to rise up in the ranks to be approved for field assignments.

The alarm rang and the speaker rang through the room to remind us that it is "combat time," and we had to go to our class by ages. We went into the battle room and knelt down ready to see the first fight of the day. The sensei called two students, one named Aidan Kuzumaki and another kid in our class. Once the sensei gave Aidan the blindfold, everything was going to change...

TO BE CONTINUED: SOON!!!

WHEN THE COMPLETE NOVEL RELEASES!!!

About the Author

Isiss Proby is currently a college student, who is driven to continue to write more stories. Also, her current book is in the works to be released soon.

Fifty-One-Fifty

Kayghee Reynolds

"I have shed so many tears

For all my failures

And I'm all dried out"

~Kayghee Reynolds

A cold sweat broke out over Heather's face as she sat in the tiny dilapidated room and listened to her mother, Cindy, argue with the doctors. Cindy was a dark-skinned Latina, with thick coarse black hair that curled all the way down to her mid-back. Heather, with her pale skin and hazel eyes, obviously didn't inherit much of her mother's coloring. She got her looks from her Scottish father, along with his height. He was not there, because he had to take care of the house and make sure her younger brother, Brad, got to school. Heather didn't mean to become such a burden on her family. Honestly, she hadn't planned on being anything. She had swallowed countless pills and alcohol in an attempt to cease to exist. Giving up always seemed very tempting to Heather, but it became the only answer when school, a broken heart, and one too many deaths in the family finally became too much. This all led to this small room with the broken ceiling tiles and dirty walls. It was the reason her mom questioned why she had to be here.

"It is mandatory for people like her to be put on a 72-hour watch," said the man sitting behind the desk.

"But why does she need to stay here? Is there no place else?" Cindy's furrowed brow and disgusted pout gave away how truly uncomfortable she was leaving her only daughter in such a place.

"Ma'am, we are the only outpatient facility with a youth ward in Orange County. If you do not have her voluntarily put in here, we will be forced to make her stay, and it will end up on her record for life." The doctor kept his stern eyes on Heather the entire time.

Cindy knew there was nothing she could do, so she had her daughter's possessions checked in at the front. Heather watched silently as her stuff was poked and prodded. Then, her bear came out of the bag. It was a cute bear with light tan fur, a pink nose, and a bow to match.

"Either, we cut off the ribbon, or you can't have the bear with you," the bulky stoic orderly stated.

"But... why?" Heather loved how sweet the bow made her bear look and helped add to the irony of its name, Killer.

"It can be used as a weapon and as a way to hang yourself, so it has to go." The scissors in his hands seemed to shine menacingly as he spoke. Heather nodded to cut the ribbon and felt her privacy cut away with it.

Cindy kissed and hugged Heather good bye and was escorted away. Another orderly came and grabbed the approved items she had brought and walked her to her shared room. The four walls were a startling white. One had a small window that looked into the play area and another wall had the entrance with no door. The policy of no doors was so patients could either off themselves or anyone else. The only room where patients were allowed to be alone and have a door was the shower/bathroom, but there were no locks. Heather put what she had either on the bed or into the drawer she was given that was under her nightstand. The orderly stood in the entrance way until she was done unpacking. Heather turned to the short woman and informed her she was done. The woman waived for Heather to follow, and they began a rather short tour of the tiny wing that would be her home for the next three days.

"This is the main room. You'll have down time in here, class, group therapy session and in the back room is where you'll have your one-on-one session with the doctor. My name is Rose. If you need anything, just come see us at the desk. Don't go outside or into your room unless instructed, and you need to ask us to escort you to the bathroom." The orderly told Heather to mingle with the other patients and bobbed away.

There were five other people scattered in the room: two boys and three girls, all between the ages of 14-17. Over at the table talking, there was a shy young girl with long brown hair, a black hoodie, and a look of dread. She was being talked at and she didn't seem to be responding back to a boy with scraggly hair and a look that makes you question if he belonged to the wing next door with the permanent residences. On the couch was a large boy laughing at a movie with a long-legged girl who almost snorted the water out of her nose that she was drinking. Heather pulled up a chair at a different table and faced the TV. It looked like they were watching Benchwarmers and were about halfway through. Heather had seen the movie a million times. So, instead, she focused her attention on the couch. It was "L" shaped, made of a leather that was an unattractive dark green color and looked like it had seen the end of World War II.

"Hello!" A curvy girl plopped down in front of Heather and interrupted her analysis of that ugly old couch.

"Um... Hello."

"My name is Shandra! I've been here since yesterday. I basically know everything there needs to be known about this place. I saw you had family bring you. That's nice. My family didn't find out 'til this morning. They kinda suck. Did your mom put you in her because she didn't wanna deal with you or what? You don't look like the crazy type or really the drug type. Why are you here?" She almost didn't take a breath during her whole introduction.

Heather blinked deliberately and slowly as she tried to decipher what Shandra had just said. "Uh… no. My family didn't really put me in here. I did it when I tried to kill myself with a handful of pills."

"Me too!" Spit flew out of her mouth, luckily missing Heather completely. "I tried to off myself by overdosing on meth, but that obviously didn't work out. I am tired of my fucking family. Wanna see a picture of my baby? Look…" She pulled out a black and white wrinkled picture from her pocket. "See? He's got my hair, but he's got my daddy's eyes. Yeah, that's my daddy's baby, but Momma won't believe me. She says I'm a liar. So, I left and tried to kill myself, but I sure do miss my baby. I love that baby more than I love me!"

Shandra rambled on 'til two orderlies walked in with a large collection of trays and announced lunchtime. Every gray tray had a little piece of paper with a name and any dietary accommodations scribbled at the very bottom. Heather remembered filling out paperwork earlier stating she was a vegetarian. When she got her plate and opened it up, there was a simple salad and a PB&J sandwich. She sat at the table where everyone else had already started working on their meals. The girl who was sitting there earlier still hadn't gotten up to get her plate. The bulky orderly from before came over.

"Sara, you need to come grab your plate." He waited for any signs of life. "Please."

Her eyes shifted to the cart, and she got up slowly. Her hair seemed to move on its own when she walked, and her arms did not swing, which was very unnerving and beautiful. When she sat back down with her tray, Heather's stare was met with her black eyes. Heather glanced away quickly and locked eyes with the boy who was talking to Sara earlier, now on the opposite side of the table.

"Hello, my name is Hank. His gentle beast is George. I saw you meet Shandra earlier. That's Sara, and finally, this is Miss Charlotte. What is your name, Madame?" Heather gagged on how sweet his voice was.

"My name is Heather. Nice to meet you all officially." She actually hated meeting new people. It was painful to make small talk and pretend to care about what people have to say.

"Hi, Heather. I hope you don't mind me asking, but why are you here?" George had a deep rich voice that really needed only to be above a whisper to hear.

"I don't mind. I tried to commit suicide by swallowing a handful of pills. I was at the hospital for three days, and now, I am here for another three." Her story was one she didn't mind sharing. Her life was an open book; but one only needed to ask.

"I think most of us are in here for that, except for Charlotte. She tried to stab someone when she took a shot of heroine, but she's cool now. I am leaving tonight actually; just got done with my three-day hold and am waiting on my parents to show up." Hank smiled like he won a triathlon as he said the last sentence. He did have something to be proud of.

As the group continued to talk, Heather learned a little bit more about each of them. Hank tried killing himself because of the pressure to be perfect at sports, school and life in general. When his parents showed up yesterday to visit, he explained the mounting pressure he felt from them. They all cried and hugged it out; his parents had no idea they were doing that to him and promised to be better. They told him how at sixteen, they shouldn't put that much weight on his shoulders. Charlotte had some anger issues that ended with her trying to stab a friend at school because her friend won a game of handball. She was the youngest of all, at the age of fourteen. She had a lot of issues with controlling her emotions in general and told the group how that wasn't exactly her first time in a psych hold. George tried hanging himself. The bullying and name calling from being a larger guy was too much for his sweet heart to handle. Similarly, his weight was too much for the rope and fan to handle, which is why his grandma found him.

The group continued talking, except Sara. She hadn't said a word the whole time, and before Heather could ask her any questions, they called the group together for a group therapy session. They all gathered the chairs in a circle and waited. Hank grabbed an extra for the therapist who was arriving shortly. When she entered the room, Heather was intrigued because of her clothing. She was wearing jeans, a regular t-shirt and a blazer. Her hair was in a messy ponytail, and her glasses were rimless. Everyone stayed quiet as she got settled into her spot and opened her black soft leather brief case.

"Hello, everyone. I see we have a new face! My name is Stephanie Gunderson. You may call me Dr. Gunderson. What is your name and can you tell us a little about yourself?" That question came up a lot that day, and Heather honestly thought about wearing a nametag to prevent it from coming up again.

"Hello, my name is Heather. I am a seventeen-year-old senior at Sonora High School. I play the trumpet in band, and I am chronically depressed." She made her voice sound like she was at an AA meeting.

"Thank you, Miss Heather. Today's activity is about your inner bully. I'm going to pass out this story and have you all read it to yourself." Dr. Gunderson passed out the papers and waited as they all sat quietly and read it internally. Once all of their heads popped up again, she explained the assignment.

"In this story, you learn about a girl who is beaten and bullied by someone who is following her around. By the end, you come to find out that her bully was her internal voice the whole time. I am passing around another piece of paper. This time it is blank. I would like you to take a pen and write down three things your inner bully tells you. When you are done, please put your pen down." This time, instead of waiting, Dr. Gunderson pulled out her own pen and wrote down her own list of three. Heather scribbled down her list: I am dumb, I am not good enough, and I am unimportant.

"Now that everyone is done writing down their list, I want you to pick a buddy and swap papers. There is an odd number. So, Heather, I would like to swap with you, and you can swap my paper with someone else." Dr. Gunderson hands Heather her paper, and Heather gave the doctor hers.

"Okay, everyone have someone else's? Good. What I would like everyone to do is say those things to the person who wrote them like you are the inner voice. Ready?" Dr. Gunderson faced Heather and began repeating the list back to her.

"You fail at everything, you are dumb, you are not good enough, and you are unimportant." Heather felt tears in her eyes hearing those things being said aloud.

"Alright, everyone. Bring it back. My question for everyone is how did that make you feel? Would you ever let someone talk to you like that?" Everyone shook their head. "Wouldn't you want to kick that person's ass?" This time people nodded and grunted in agreement. "So why is it... that it's okay for you to say that to yourself?" The group sat quietly, most of them still reeling from that mind-blowing revelation.

"Your next task is to write down something positive based off the list of the other person. Please put your pen down when you are done." Again, everyone looked down and scribbled away. Heather tried doing her best, but positive spins were not her thing. "Now, please read what you wrote to the other person." Dr. Gunderson faced Heather and said, "You do great just the way you are. You are brilliant, you are good enough, and you are so special."

Heather's eyes welled up, and her mind drifted off. She had only ever been so mean and abusive to herself. In the story, the girl gave her inner voice a name. It was the name of someone who had tormented her for years. So, who would hers be? For the longest time, she blamed her mother, but her mother was so loving and encouraging that the title of bully did not fit her. Thinking back deep into her mind, she remembered living with a girl named Lauren, who was a nasty thing that always told her things like, remember to suck in your belly so you don't look so fat and no one wants to be your friend. Lauren was the voice of her inner bully, and Heather planned on kicking her out.

"That will be all. Have a wonderful rest of the day." Dr. Gunderson said as she packed her things, then left.

About the same time she exited, the orderlies, the bulky male and the tiny female from earlier, entered the room with the cart of trays. Everyone moved their chairs back to where they belonged and got in line for food, all except Hank, who had basically burst out of the room when he saw his parents at the desk filling out the final paper work to release him. He came back and hugged them all; then, he left to pack his things. Sara was a little bit more proactive in getting her food and actually giggled when Heather tripped and nearly threw her food everywhere. Once they were all seated, they talked about what they had learned in group.

"Fuck my inner bully, man! I'd kill her if I could!" Charlotte spat out in between chewing her Salisbury steak.

"I really liked the exercise! It helped me better understand what I say in my mind isn't truth! When I get home, I'm gonna tell my momma and daddy and my baby! My baby won't really understand but hopefully he'll internalize it and he'll be better for it. I know there is stuff we live our lives by that we don't even remember and the same will go for my baby. Mhm, he won't remember me telling him, but I would have said it, so that's all that matters!" Heather was impressed by Shandra's ability to speak and eat. She should become one of those people that works at auctions and sells the items.

"I think I got a lot out of it. If I can stop my inner bully, maybe the outer bully's words won't hurt so much." George hadn't even touched his food yet, but he was pretty good about waiting between forkfuls to say something.

"Me too. What about you, Sara?" Heather wanted to get her involved.

"Eh. It was cool." Sara's voice was very monotone but still captured the attention of everyone around her.

Once dinner and the conversation were done, the patients were allowed to hang out or take a shower before bed. Heather was one for morning showers, so she walked over to the tall long desk and talked to Mr. Bulky.

"Hello."

"Hello, ma'am. What can I do for you?"

"I just kind of want to talk." She looked at his name badge and saw it said Eric.

"Oh, okay. How are you today? Heather, right?"

"I'm alright, could be better, and yes, it's Heather. I miss having paper and pens to draw."

"You like drawing? Me too. I do more graffiti art though. I can't get you a pen but we have paper and crayons for you guys."

"I do and would love a crayon or two. Can you draw me something?"

"Alright, follow me." He got up and had her follow him to the main room. "I can draw you something. Like what?"

"My name would be a cool thing." He showed her where the plastic bin was that held all of the art supplies; it was very similar to a kindergarten class, minus the scissors. "Thanks!"

"Not a problem, and consider it done!"

Eric left Heather to doodle, which she did for a long while before it was lights out. When it was time for bed, Heather cleaned up the mess she made and walked to her room. It turned out her roommate was Sara. She had just taken a shower and was combing her hair when Heather came in.

"Sara, can I ask why you are in here?"

"Similar reasons to you. Just a different method." Sara flashed her two rather large barely healing scars on her arms. "They found me in my room. My boy scout of a brother kept me from bleeding out 'til the paramedics showed up."

"Wow, was it your first time?"

"This is my third time in here in a month. My new tactic is to stop eating, but that's a hard one to do."

Sara and Heather talked most of the night about their stories 'til Eric had to finally come in and hush them up. Though she felt very alone and scared when she showed up, Heather actually felt more connected to other human beings than she ever had before. The black room around her welcomed her sleepy eyes to shut as she thought of that and her new much more positive look on the future before her.

About the Author

Kayghee has been writing for eleven years, but this is her first short story. Her main love can is poetry, because she likes to get her ideas out in as few words as possible. Kayghee grew up in small town La Habra, CA and graduated from one of the high schools. While there, she joined the band and a medical academy to start a career in the medical field. After her four years in the program were up, she decided she wanted to actually study psychology. This led her to Fullerton College where she has been taking her classes for general education and for her psychology major.

Outside of school, she is heavily involved with the Boy Scouts of America as an adult leader in a troop, crew and OA chapter. She herself has gone through the program and earned the Silver award in her crew. Along with scouting, she likes to spend her spare time painting, hanging out with her friends and reading. She hopes to one day make a career out of her art and writing.

A Touch of Paradise

Gary Rodriguez

"It is better to have your head in the clouds, and know where you are... than to breathe the clearer atmosphere below them, and think that you are in paradise."

Henry David Thoreau

"Is this safe?" I ask my friend as we try to navigate a safe path to descend the ridge we are on.

"Sure, I know these mountains like the back of my hand," the man says.

"Good. I don't think I could climb down the way the others did with this guitar case in my hand." Then, just as soon as he assures me it was safe... Crash! Whack! The dust and ash fly, as two guys tumble and slide down a fire-stricken slope in an avalanche fashion. As we tumble, I hold onto my guitar case for dear life, as I crash into several charred trees in the area. After hitting the bottom, I say to myself, *Where's my guitar case?* Click, click. My friend turns his head to the direction of the clicking sound.

"Watch out!" he tries to motion to me with a panicked look on his face. As he looks helplessly, I immediately recall that my guitar case is no longer in my hand. Then as if by an angel's divine protective instinct, I thrust my right arm backwards catching the twenty-pound hardwood guitar case like a football quarterback in the process of releasing the ball. And, after briefly catching it, I guide the guitar case a solid ten feet in front of me. All this occurred in under a minute. Still filled with adrenaline, I try to get ahold of myself.

Then, after taking a few breaths, I look at my friend to gain confirmation that he is all right. My friend is a tall lengthy man of about six feet. He has brown hair, dark brown eyes, and is covered in sand and ash from the fall.

"Thanks for the warning, Rob," I say. Rob gives a quick glance over at me seeing that I too am covered in ash and sand.

"You all right, Gary?" he laughs for a second and thinks to himself, *Of course, he is. I mean he's built like a football player.*

After laughing at our helplessness, he stands up. I myself still covered in sand and ash begin to stand up and shake the dirt out of my dark brown hair. As I position myself, I lean forward reaching my hands into the dirt before me to notice that it is very soft. While getting up I ponder to myself, *Why is the dirt was soft like sand?* Once up, I turn around to see the dust cloud slowly rise and dissipate. Then, as if the moon wants to illuminate our path, the clouds depart from the moon bringing light to our surroundings. We look up towards our previous position. This makes us realize why what had occurred had occurred. Ash and charred trees filled the side of the hill from where we had fallen.

Being flabbergasted and bamboozled, we retrace our steps. Climbing up the hill, I notice which path I had fallen from. I am confident to say the least, because there is a trail of busted and broken tree branches everywhere. The destructive scene was caused by my guitar case while it was in my hand. After carefully analyzing the scene of the fall, we look at each other and conclude what happened. There before us, on the ground, was a giant rock, which had crumbled into two. While on the ridge, we figured that the rock was not charred.

"It must have been weak from the fire three months ago," he said. Feeling lucky, we joke that death had dumped me and cancelled our date that night. We then proceed to meet with our other friends who had been on their way to the meeting point. As we proceed on to our rendezvous point with the group, I close my eyes to remember just how I got here.

It was ten o'clock in the morning and summer vacation. Like all young guys my age, I was sleeping. I had nothing to do, nothing planned, and expected nothing eventful to happen.

While I slept, however, others were not thinking the way I was. "Guess who just got back today? Those wild-eyed boys that had been away haven't changed, haven't much to say. But man, I still think those cats are great" (The ringtone is playing the song of the Thin Lizzy's "The Boys Are Back in Town"). By the time the song finished that line, I had awakened.

I rustled out of the thin white sheets that were on my bed and reached for my cell, which was on my dresser. "Hello?" I answered with a deep baritone voice, crust in my eyes and a hairstyle that looked like I came out of a tornado.

"Gary!" The voice answered back. "I have a proposition for you." I lifted my head with my eyes half opened and said, "Well, since you've disturbed me from my hibernation, I might as well hear you out."

The voice continued and said, "I just got the okay from my mom to take you, me, Rich, Mendez, and Chris up to Porter Ranch for the week. Can you go?" At that point, I looked up at my screen to see whom I was speaking to. The screen read Rob Salazar. *Figures as much coming from Rob,* I said to myself.

"What time are we meeting and where?" I asked him.

"We will meet up at Rich's house at 14 hundred hours."

"Sounds good," I replied. The phone call ended and left me curious. What could Rob have planned that could take up a whole week and on top of all that at his mom's place? Getting out of bed, I chuckled to myself at the very idea that whatever he had planned it must be crazy. He's pretty smart, too smart for his own good sometimes. It's kind of funny. Aside from his intelligence, he also possesses the necessary skills to be an outstanding leader. Actually, everyone in this group possessed similar traits, which is probably the reason why we all get along well.

After pondering the numerous events that may take place, I sprung myself from the bed and began to gather all the materials needed for the trip. I filled my duffle bag up to bursting with clothes, hygienic materials, and medication. Then, another thought hit me. I'm getting ready to embark on this journey, and I haven't even told my folks yet. How are they going to react to my sudden leave of absence? I come from a family that likes parental control, even though I am adult by age. And from past experience, I've learned that they like to be in charge of when I departed and returned. Their control doesn't sit well with me though, as I am a free-spirited kind of guy. So, I shall tell them on my way out the door.

One thirty rolled around, and the doorbell rang. I told my parents I'd be gone for a week, and my ride was already outside. They weren't too pleased, but they also never like to keep others waiting. I know I'll hear it later, but I'll handle that problem when I reach it. As I walked out, I greeted my friend Chris. Chris is about as tall as I am at about five eleven, looks kinda Indian with his Moreno-colored skin, has dark brown eyes, long black hair, and has the athletic build of a runner. After we greeted one another with a signature handshake, I realized I didn't have my guitar.

"We can't have good road trip without music. Can we?" I said to Chris.

"Nope, unless you want us to be extremely bored out of our freakin' minds up there," he said very sarcastically. Chris is also a musician like me; I know he understood my needs. After grabbing my black Yamaha guitar case, we left in his van.

As we pulled up to Rich's house, we saw our crew of friends grabbing their supplies and shoving them into a Jeep. It had been awhile since the crew last got together, maybe three months at the least. As we gather our stuff from the van, we yell, "Mendez! As he turned around, we notice his gear is stacked higher than he is.

"Little high, little low," I yelled to Mendez, but only to receive a spiteful, "Shut up" and a middle finger. Mendez is a short guy about five seven in height, kinda nerdy looking, clean cut, with black hair and eyes. Running out of the house was Rich yelling, "Hurry up. We're on a time limit, guys. And, we don't want to keep our ride waiting." He is about as tall as Chris and I, a ginger kid, red hair, blue eyes, clean cut and built like a runner. He never likes to be late, so he helped us pack the last of our supplies into the Jeep.

"Umm, how are all gonna fit inside the car with all this stuff?" I asked.

"Well, two people are going to have to sit in the trunk with all the stuff. Just duck your heads if you see the police," Rob said.

"I vote Chris and Mendez!" Rich yells. Then, they look to me.

"I ain't going back there. I'm too big," I said.

"Well, on the way back one of you's is gonna sit in the trunk," Chris said. Laughing at Chris, Mendez said, "I'm short and can fit like a contortionist." With that being settled, Chris and Mendez sat in the trunk. After we settled ourselves in like Tetris blocks, Rob introduced us to his mom and sister. He then also went on to talk about how he and Rich had been planning the trip for a couple of days but barely decided to inform us a couple of hours prior to our trip.

After everything was said and settled, we departed for Porter Ranch to spend our week. The car ride was pretty boring and offered little excitement. However, it was a bit funny when Chris and Mendez would hide from California Highway Patrol officers every time one was spotted. Altogether, the ride last a little over three hours. When we finally reached our destination, everyone except for Rob, his mom, and his sister were in shock. What we saw was an isolated area with a full security staff on post and nice beautiful houses everywhere.

At that point, we knew Rob's mom had money. After rounding the corner, we pulled into the driveway and unpacked ourselves. We were like stuffed sardines packed tightly. Well, everyone except for Chris and Mendez. They were packed in the trunk like an over-filled closet ready to explode. I jokingly said to them, "Are you ready to be released from your eternal imprisonment?!"

"YES!" they chorused, as I laughed and pulled the lever of their freedom. The trio of Rob, Rich, and myself burst into a thunderous laughter with tears trailing down our faces. Then, looking down at our stiff legs, we laughed some more. By that time, Chris and Mendez got out of the car very awkwardly; their legs had gone into a deep slumber. As they stood up, their legs began to tremble like a one-year-old child learning how to walk. Our laughter went from a hysterical funny laugh to a painful laugh, as we held onto our stomachs.

After we finished our laughing, I turned around to see the house. Rob's house was a beautiful two-story house. It had dark green grass, small palm trees stationed at the four corners of the yard, lights all around the driveway, and a running water fountain with an angel on top. After my brief adoration of the house, I gathered my gear and followed the group inside. The inside is like what you'd expect from anybody well off: lots of furniture, beautiful paintings on the walls, a nice kitchen, and a big T.V. with a loud surround sound. After we got inside, we dropped off our stuff off in Rob's room.

"GO CHANGE!" Rob's mom yelled from the kitchen. "WE HAVE A POOL OUTSIDE!" Rob forgot to mention that he had a pool; luckily, I had packed gym shorts just in case. In any event, we all gathered our swimwear and headed outside. By that time, it was about seven in the evening, the weather was fair, and the backyard looked like a scene taken out of a movie, one where there was a small oasis in the middle of nowhere with a small waterfall. After another awe-inspiring view, I turned my attention towards the fence and viewed what lay beyond it. As I approached the fence to see exactly where we were, I was again awe stricken. What I saw was the city of Los Angeles. I could see the big buildings, the street lights, cars driving through the streets; I had never seen L.A. like that before.

Once my experience had ended, I turned around to see Rob's mom and stepdad, and by the looks of things, it was time for introductions. Other than our brief meeting on the ride there, I had paid little attention to what she actually looked like. She was in shape and obviously a woman who took care of herself, had dirty blond hair and dark brown eyes, and was Caucasian like Rob. Her husband Mike was also in shape, rather tall and was African American. Once finished with their introductions, they lay down the rules of their home: "Don't let the children go near the water unsupervised, don't be too loud, you're welcome to feed yourself, and have a good time while you're here." Rob's younger siblings were not there at the time, so that was one thing to mark off for that night.

With that, we all jumped into the pool. I immediately grabbed Chris and submerged him underwater. *That was probably a bad idea,* I thought to myself. Then all of a sudden, Chris gets out from under me and pulls me under. *Crap!* I thought it was definitely a bad idea. I can't swim that well. The rough housing went on for a little while then died off. By that time, it was around 7:45. We were in paradise. I felt really free and safe, and it was my assumption that we'd stay there the rest of the night, but I was about to be proven otherwise. 8:30 rolled around, and we had made our way to the Jacuzzi waterfall. We sat there and just soaked up the heat. It was a nice change and very relaxing.

"So, there are mountains near here that I've been exploring, and I know the perfect spot to camp," Rob says. We look around at each other and thought to ourselves, *Rob has never done anything that was an extremely bad idea, except maybe when he convinced us to ditch in high school. That almost got us caught by the police.*

"Sure, why not!" we replied. With our decisions made, we got out and dressed for the soon to come event. *A list,* I thought.

"What do we need, Rob?" I asked.

"Well, since it will only take about 20 minutes to get there, we shall take a flashlight, a tent, and one sleeping bag to lie on. It's summer. Who needs to be covered anyways?" He chuckled as he said these things.

I grabbed a few bags of Top Ramen and some water, just in case. I like to be prepared. Oh, and my trusty guitar. Then came our final obstacle. It was nine o'clock in the evening and there we were, a bunch of young adults, about to embark on a journey in camouflaged gear.

"Where are you all going?" Rob's mom asked.

"We're going in those mountains behind the block to camp," Rob said proudly.

"Don't you know it's unsafe to travel in the mountains?" Rob's mom commented.

I felt that was a good time to jump in, "This might sound crazy, but I can ensure the group's safety." I was the oldest, so it seemed right to do so. After careful consideration, Rob's mom finally gave the okay on the account that we text her upon arrival and our return in the morning, or she would send a search team.

With matters settled, we made our way to the security post. Upon arriving at the post, we got strange looks and a few chuckles from the guards. Looking back, I probably would have laughed at us too. What they saw was a rag tag group of kids who looked like they were dressed to play in a Vietnam War movie, accompanied by a guitarist. As you might have noticed by now, we were military geeks, and that felt like a mission, a mission to infiltrate the hills and scout out the area. Without any objections, they let us go.

We must have walked for about ten minutes until we came across an opening near the hills. There was sand and wild life everywhere. Ten minutes passed, and we reached the base of the hill. The hill looked steep and would obviously prove to be a tough climb. At that point in time, small clouds began to cover the moon limiting our light.

"What now, Rob, no light?" Rich and Mendez asked. Rob chuckled at their uncertainty and shaken resolve; then, he pulled out a five-inch LED flashlight.

"Here's your light!" he said while laughing lightly to himself.

"Well, we're already this far, so we might as well keep going," Chris and I said. Waiting to get the approval from Mendez and Rich, we looked back to them, but see they were still a bit uncertain of the small LED flashlight.

"We just have one flashlight, and this doesn't seem to be a good idea," Rich said.

"Nonsense!" Rob said as he turned on the flashlight to prove to us the distance it could illuminate. If I would have to take a guess on the distance, I would estimate anywhere from eight hundred to a thousand feet. With everyone on board, we ascended up the steep hill. Then about 200 feet in, I slipped and fell. And, as I began falling, Rich, who was in front of me, turned around and caught me by my guitar case.

"Whew! That was a close one," Rich said.

"Yeah. Thanks. I would have taken a nasty fall if it weren't for that." After that small incident, we continued the climb with Rob leading the way. We must have climbed that hill for fifteen minutes, until we reached the top. The top was filled with brush and wild trees. Human alteration was nowhere to be seen.

Then out of nowhere, we heard the sound of coyotes howling out in the distant. Thump, thump, I could feel my heart rate start to rise as I looked around to see if any coyotes were near. Snap! Crack! We turned our heads quickly to our right in a desperate effort to locate the sound. Then, after a few seconds of silence, two jack rabbits raced out of the brush chasing each other. Wow! We chorused. All that for a couple of jack rabbits? Our pulses were a little high after that, as we laughed at our frightened selves.

After confirming nothing else was near, we proceeded. The path we took kind of resembled a trail or maybe a dried-up stream. Either way, it was a solid path to take uninterrupted by the brush. About five minutes into the walk, we heard the howls again, and due to the hollowness of the hills, the sound bounced off the rocks leaving us unable to determine their location. *The howls brought about a sense of excitement,* I thought to myself as we continued to walk.

"Wait! Stop!" The immediate halt was unexpected and caused us to bump into each other.

"Why did we stop, Rob?" I said from the back of the group. Curiously, I made way to the front of the group. There before me was a cliff with no sign of an end. The darkness made it seem ominous.

"Oh, yeah. I forgot to mention the big drop that was here. I always come in the daytime, so the lighting is never a problem. The drop is only about a hundred feet." Rob laughed. After viewing the fall, Rob pointed to our destination down below about one hundred yards away.

"Great. I bring a guitar, and now I gotta climb this cliff."

"It's easy," Rob exclaimed and handed the light over to Rich who was doubtful. "Shine the light on me as I climb down," Rob said while he descended.

Laughing, Chris and Mendez yell, "You make it look so easy!"

Rob laughing from below, "It is. Your turn, Chris."

"Screw it," Chris said as he descended. After him descended, Mendez followed. Now the only people on the ridge are Rich and I, along with and all of our supplies. Rich, paranoid at the situation he got into began to descend saying, "If I fall, I'm suing all of you!"

"That is if we don't leave you there first!" Mendez yelled and laughed hard with Rob and Chris.

Now it's my turn, I thought. "How the hell am I gonna get down there with my guitar?"

"Toss all the stuff down, including your guitar!" Rob yelled up to me.

"Are you crazy?" Chris and Rich yell. "That thing is heavy!"

Overruled by the majority's decision, Rob climbed back up. "I know another way that might be easier," Rob said.

"Screw you, Rob," Rich yelled. "You could have showed us that way instead." After that, we tossed the supplies to them, excluding my guitar.

"Set up the tent in that sandy area out there," Rob yelled. We then began to walk towards a ridge that was about 90 feet away. As soon as we reached it- Crash! Whack! As I opened my eyes, I am reminded with scattered evidence as to how I finally got here from the fall.

Where would I be had I not picked up my phone this morning? I thought. *I sure as hell wouldn't be here.*

With a moonlit path before us, Rob and I proceeded down the slope. However, we descend safely. After dusting ourselves off, we went to meet up with the guys.

"You're a freakin' idiot, Rob," Rich yelled.

"What? Why?"

"That?!" Knowing why Rich was pointing, he laughed. Curious myself, I looked to the side where Rich was pointing, and I didn't believe what I saw. The entrance we saw on our way up there was our final destination! Ten minutes from where Rob lived was our actual destination. By that time, Rob was laughing hysterically, and it caught like wild fire as we all start dying of laughter.

"Don't be mad. What's the point of taking the easier route? There's no fun involved!" Rob yelled.

"First, you decided on this crazy idea of camping in the mountains. Then, you take us past our destination on purpose, and on top of all that, you almost got me and everyone else killed!" At that point, we burst out in laughter at the dangerous adventure we just embarked on. I look back at Rich with watering eyes to see that he was dumbfounded still. Then, Rich gave in and started laughing at it too saying, "Screw you guys!"

Well, if there's anything I can take from that adventure is taking the easy route may get you to your location quicker, but taking the hard way will give you memories that you'll always remember. Quoting the great American poet Robert Frost, "Two roads diverged in a wood, and I--I took the one less traveled by, and that has made all the difference."

Still, this is only the first night. I wonder what Rob has planned for tomorrow....

About the Author

Gary Rodriguez is a young native of San Bernardino who is currently studying Business Management at the University of Phoenix's San Bernardino Campus. His goals for the next two years include gaining experiences in marketing, writing, and attaining his Bachelor's degree. His passions include singing opera, writing poetry, writing Bach style Chorales, and playing guitar. Gary is also an active musician in the community and often performs with the San Bernardino Valley College Music Department, local community centers, and in his church.

My Grandma's Stolen Car

Jena Snapp

"Trust takes years to build, seconds to break, and forever to repair."

Unknown Author

It was just another day, and I was visiting my family at my grandma's house after school. As I drove up to the house, I noticed there was no one parked in the driveway. I laughingly thought to myself, *Sweet! Front row parking!* After parking my little black car, I meandered into the house. Without skipping a beat, I wandered straight into my grandma's room. As I sat on her bed, my grandma asked about my day, and we nonchalantly discussed the weather. I started to get hungry, so I made my way to her kitchen. The kitchen was under construction, which meant I had to tactfully walk around Jack, our family friend, as he worked on the flooring. Jack and his friend Aaron had been working on the hefty project for the past week. That day was different. That day, Jack was working alone. Once my stomach was full of the very yummy, crunchy, and sweet honeycomb cereal, I decided to go upstairs to visit with the rest of my family. I visited my old home nearly every day, so that was no extraordinary event. After the mention of honeycombs to my mom, she went downstairs for some as well. While I was still upstairs, I heard my mom's worrisome, panicked voice asking, "Where is Grandma's car?" The mood instantaneously changed.

Because my grandma could no longer drive herself, she graciously lent out her car to my aunt. My aunt would run errands for my grandma in exchange for utilizing the car whenever she needed it. Everyone who noticed my grandma's car was absent, including me, assumed my aunt was once again borrowing it. My mom was the only who thought to mention it to my grandma. My grandma quickly responded in agitation, "What do you mean? Isn't it in the driveway?" That's when my grandma realized someone had brazenly stolen her gold 1992 Cadillac Catera straight from her driveway. She promptly called the police to begin a police report. All I could think about was, who in the world would steal my sweet loving grandma's car. As I watched the hurt and worry in her eyes, I began to well up with anger towards the person who did that to her. I needed to find out who it was. I started to analyze the whole day to find some type of abnormality that could lead to a clue. I thought about pulling into the driveway and quickly began to feel remorse. The thought of her car being stolen did not even cross my mind. I next thought about Jack's friend, Aaron, who was helping with my grandma's flooring. Aaron was mysteriously gone that day. I wanted to mention his name as a potential suspect, but I felt bad about accusing someone I hardly knew.

I noticed Jack in the backyard completely avoiding everyone during the time of the situation. Typically, one would assume anyone's response would be that of concern and/or surprise. Jack was neither of these. He looked as if he was scared and tried to stay away. I didn't mention Jack's reaction either. I thought I was just overreacting. Why was I so quick to blame a seemingly innocent man? About an hour later, I went to my grandma's room. She had just finished her phone call with the police. She began to tell me that Aaron was asking her the day before about the two cars in the driveway and asked if either of them ran. She told him only one of them did and that was her car. She thought he was interested in buying the car, so she told him all about it. Aaron had been working for my grandma for about a week. She didn't know much about him other than he was Jack's friend and needed work. Jack had been around our family for as long as I could remember, so my grandma trusted Jack.

My grandma and I decided to question Jack about Aaron. We asked if he knew where Aaron was. Jack said they were drinking together the night before and Aaron gotten extremely drunk. Jack assumed Aaron's hangover was the cause of his absence. I told my grandma about my suspicions about Aaron- a man we hardly knew who was asking about her car, then not showing up to work the day the car goes missing. It didn't exactly sound like a coincidence. We told the police everything, but at that point, there wasn't much they could do without physical evidence. A few days passed by, and I was on my daily trip to my family's home. I drove past a neighbor's house and noticed Jack's car parked out front.

I, being my quizzical self, slowed down to see him out front with some friends. They were taking shots, smoking, and laughing. I sped up and went to my grandma's house thinking nothing suspicious about the scene. I walked in and noticed the flooring was not even close to being finished. I asked my grandma about the project, and she said Jack had not been helping her much. She said he wasn't even answering his phone when she called. He had told her he would be there in the morning, but he never showed. My heart started pounding, and the mood quickly changed. I said to her, "I know exactly why he's not answering your phone calls. He's over at the neighbor's house slamming shots down." I wouldn't have been so quick to tell my grandma about Jack's escapades if she didn't already pay him for the full job.

I went over to the neighbor's house to speak with Jack and tell him how disrespectful he was being to my grandma. Jack had every petty excuse in the book as to why he was there and why he was not answering his phone. In his drunken words, he confessed he knew "details" about my grandma's stolen car and he would be coming by later to tell her. I went back to my grandma's to tell her he'd be coming by. After about four hours of waiting for Jack, he finally came drunkenly sauntering up the driveway. We called the police, so they'd be there to hear the details, but they took a long time to come. We sat out on the front porch as the sun began to set. Jack told us how Aaron took my grandma's keys from her purse. He knew about the theft but didn't mention it until the liquid courage flowed through his veins.

Weeks later, my grandma received a phone call saying her car was found in Victorville. The police said the car was stripped and completely totaled. Aaron was left as a suspect and never faced any charges. As for Jack, he was never welcomed back to my grandma's home again and lost the honor of being a "family friend." The whole situation was distressing and disappointing to my grandma. Thankfully, my dad felt empathy towards her and decided to finish the kitchen project at no cost. My grandma is the nicest, kindest, and most trusting person you can meet, but that encounter gave her a reality check. Remember that no matter how long you've known a person, he/she can still be dishonest. She learned to be careful about letting people get too close without fully knowing their character.

About the Author

Jena Rose Snapp flourished in a small, quaint town called Yucaipa, in Southern California for most of her life. She was always surrounded by family as her mom was one of fifteen children. Jena herself was the middle child with an older sister and a younger brother. She lived with her grandmother essentially her whole life. She invests her days in loving Jesus and her family, along with working two jobs, while attending school. She is also a licensed Esthetician. She is often is extremely motivated, loves people, and loves being outdoors.

It's Not a Perfect World

Dr. Cassundra White-Elliott

"Beauty in things exists merely in the mind

which contemplates them. "

David Hume's Essays, *Moral and Political* (1742)

Once upon a time, in a land that never existed, in a secluded mansion, which sat at the top of a steep winding road, was a thirty-nine year old woman, in the main parlor. The woman was no ordinary woman, not by any means. From the time she had been a teenager until her mid-30s, she had won beauty pageant after beauty pageant, and each win always came with a large sum of money. As a result, by the time she was thirty-six years old, she had become one of the wealthiest women in her local community, her state, and the neighboring states.

One evening, when the woman had been thirty-seven, her dedicated family chauffeur, of over twenty years, was driving her to one of the five-star restaurants in the downtown area, so she could meet her fiancé for dinner. As they made their way through the torrential rain, the woman began having second and third thoughts about traveling in such weather, even to see the love of her life, the man she would marry in just a few short months.

The woman was so absorbed in her thoughts that at first she was unaware that the tires of the car were skidding to the left, which caused the car to move into oncoming traffic. Before the woman realized what was occurring, the Lincoln town car in which she was riding, was sharply impacted by a Cadillac SUV. The Lincoln was fiercely pushed into the guard rail, and instead of the rail stopping the car's movement, the speed and the wet pavement caused the town car to flip over the rail and land in the ravine below.

The impact the town car received from the Cadillac caused the windows to shatter. Glass flew everywhere, including into the woman's face, leaving gashes on the right side. When the car landed in the ravine, the impact of the landing caused the car door to bend inward, jabbing the woman in her right leg, tearing her flesh open.

Feeling the jarring pain, the woman slowly began to lose consciousness. She tried fighting it, but her body was reacting to the severe pain she was experiencing, shutting itself down as a mode of preservation. In the distance, she could hear the wail of sirens and knew someone was coming to her rescue. Then, she heard her chauffeur's voice asking if she was okay. But, she could not answer, as she found herself shrouded in darkness.

When she finally came to, she was in a hospital bed, and twelve hours had passed. Shaking her head groggily, feeling the effects of the medication she had been administered, she looked around, attempting to detect her location. Before she could figure it out, she saw her fiancé sitting by the bedside. With a confused look on her face, she stared into his eyes. Noticing she was awake, he immediately began to explain what had transpired the night before during the storm, as she was making her way to meet him for dinner.

As he spoke, the woman felt something on the right side of her face. She reached up and felt a large bandage extending from the top of her cheekbone, under her eye, down to her chin. Then, she felt a sharp pain in her right leg. At that moment, the doctor walked into the room and introduced himself.

A few days later, the woman was released to go home. She was instructed to return to the hospital a few days afterward to have her wounds cleaned and her bandages replaced. After the first return hospital visit, the woman went once a week for the same treatment.

A few months later, the face bandage would be removed for the last time, and the woman would finally see the extent of her injuries. Up to that point, she had not wanted to view her face each time the nurse had offered.

Prior to going to the hospital that day, the woman had requested her fiancé's presence in the room for the unveiling. He quickly agreed to her request. He sat to her left side, holding her hand as the nurse carefully removed the bandage. Once the bandage was off, the nurse handed the woman a mirror.

Slowly, the woman lifted the mirror to her face, not really wanting to look, fearful of what she would see. As she lifted her eyes, she saw two horrors: the jagged scar that ran down her cheek and the horrified look on her fiancé's face, as he quickly rose from his chair. His abrupt change of position, from being seated to standing, caused the chair to tip backward and hit the floor with a loud thud. He mumbled, "I'll be right back." He turned and walked quickly from the room, with his hand covering his mouth. It was as if he had suddenly grown nauseous.

A tear ran down the woman's face, as she once again lifted the mirror to her face. That time, she noticed for the first time that her right eye was drooping a little. While the bandage was on, she didn't much notice what was going on with the right side of her face. She just knew she had been in a lot of pain.

The nurse excused herself and said the doctor would be in a few moments. A few minutes later, the room to the door opened again, and the woman thought it was her fiancé returning. To her disappointment, it was only the doctor coming in. He sat down and explained the options of plastic surgery to repair the scar. However, he said it would be best to wait a few months until the inner tissue healed before any further surgery was performed. The woman, dumbfounded by her fiancé's reaction, wasn't really taking in what the doctor was saying because she was wondering what was keeping her fiancé. Why was he taking so long to return? After the doctor left the room, the woman sat patiently waiting for her fiancé. She was feeling numb and lost.

After a few moments of waiting and not getting an answer when she called his cell phone, she moved from the room to the waiting area for him to come and collect her and drive her back home. Unbeknownst to her, the moment she saw the back of his head leaving the room would be the last time she would see him in her presence. Finally admitting to herself that he was not planning to return or answer her calls, she called her driver to come and pick her up from the hospital.

~~~~~~~~~~~~~~~~~

As the woman sat in the family mansion all alone, as the last surviving member of her family, she decided to go into town. It would be the first time she did so after staying home for two and a half years since the accident. She had been thoroughly humiliated when she had read in the newspaper that her engagement to a well-known bachelor had been called off. He had not had the decency to tell her himself. She was heartbroken. From that point until now, she had everything ordered in and had only allowed a few close friends to come to her home.

But, on that December morning, two days before Christmas, after the snow had ceased falling for the past few days, she had made up in her mind she would face her public, those who had once celebrated with her after each pageant in which she had been victorious. She decided she would not hide from the world any longer, and they could either accept her for who she was with the scar on her face or not. The choice would be completely theirs.

When the chauffeur pulled up outside the row of shops, the woman stepped out confidently with her head high. She was determined to go shopping to purchase gifts for the few friends who had not abandoned her and maybe a little something for herself. After being in the store for about thirty minutes, she heard a familiar voice call her name. Slowly lifting her head, the woman turned to face the man. To her surprise, it was an ex-boyfriend from college.

When he saw her face and the scar, he lifted his hand and caressed the side of her face and a tear ran down his face. The woman did not understand his emotion. She had not seen him for nearly fifteen years. She definitely did not want his pity. She attempted to step back, but he gently placed his hands on the tops of her arms and pulled her into him, embracing her.

"I have been trying to get in contact with you for years," he whispered into her ear. The woman did not respond. She did not know how to respond, so she remained silent while taking in his handsomely rugged good looks. He was still the same charming fellow he was all those years ago. That much she could tell.

"I read about the accident in the paper and the news about your engagement. I'm sorry about that. I was just so grateful to know you were okay and that you didn't marry that guy." She did not know how to take his comment. She didn't know whether she should take it personally or be flattered.

Finally, she spoke up and said, "Why were you trying to contact me?"

"I made the biggest mistake of my life when I broke up with you in college. I found that out a few years afterward. I wanted to reconnect with you."

"And now?" she questioned, as she lifted her hair from the side of her face, further exposing her scar.

"That doesn't concern me. I know the person inside. That is the person I fell in love with and have not been able to get out of my mind, even after marrying someone else."

"You're married?"

"Was. Not anymore." The man noticed a few of the other customers staring at them, so he pulled the woman into a quiet corner. "Look," he began, "give me a chance to show you that I'm not the jerk I once was." Thinking he may have been moving too fast, he asked, "Are you seeing anyone?"

With her head down, the woman said, "No," in a barely audible voice. The man placed his hand under her chin and lifted it.

"Have dinner with me tomorrow?" he asked.

"Tomorrow is Christmas Eve."

"Yes, I'm aware of that. Can we spend it together?"

With a smile on her face, the woman smiled for the first time in a very long time and responded, "Yes, that would be nice."

~~~~~~~~~~~~~~~~

At the turn of the New Year, after having spent every day since Christmas Eve with her ex, who was then her current, the woman decided to have the plastic surgery. It wasn't because she felt compelled to. No, she would do it for her new fiancé. He had not asked her to, but she wanted to be beautiful for him, both inside and outside, on the day they would say their vows, even though he had accepted her as she was when he proposed to her on Christmas Day, not wanting to take the chance of losing her again.

She had accepted his proposal and scheduled the surgery a few weeks later. After she had healed completely, they would be joined together in holy matrimony, saying their vows before a few friends and family members. The woman could not be more overjoyed with the turn of events in her life. She had wondered how things would turn out after the turmoil she had suffered through with the changes in her body and the loss of her first fiancé. She prayed for the best and truly believed in her heart that all would be well.

It just goes to show you that we don't live in a perfect world with perfect people with perfect actions. Life is what you make of it, and you must have the courage to live each day to the fullest, regardless of what the world around you thinks!

And, beauty is truly in the eyes of the beholder.

About the Editor

Dr. Cassundra White-Elliott resides in California with her family, where as an English/Education professor she teaches at various community colleges and universities.

When writing, she writes with the direction of the Holy Spirit, in an effort to share with God's people all that He has for them.

In addition to teaching and writing, Dr. White-Elliott also serves as an evangelistic teacher. She is the founder of International Women's Commission, a ministry that serves the needs of the entire person, by attending to healing the mind, body, soul, and spirit.

Dr. White-Elliott holds a Ph.D. in Education, a Master's in English Composition, and a Bachelor's in Education.

Dr. White-Elliott is also the founder of CLF Publishing, LLC. For your publishing needs, go online to www.clfpublishing.org.

Gift of Salvation
for
Non-Believers

"For all have sinned, and come short of the glory of God."
Romans 3:23

This section was written especially for non-believers, those who have not accepted the gift of salvation. The gift of salvation saves souls from eternal damnation and is a free gift offered by God himself. John 3:16-18 says, *"For God so loved the world, that he gave his only begotten Son, that whosoever believeth in him should not perish, but have everlasting life. For God sent not his Son into the world to condemn the world; but that the world through him might be saved. He that believeth on him is not condemned: but he that believeth not is condemned already, because he hath not believed in the name of the only begotten Son of God."* This section of scripture tells us God's purpose for giving His son Jesus to the world. The world was in a bad condition. The world was overwrought with sin; the people were living for fleshly desires rather than for God's desires.

As a result of the world's conditions, God decided that He would offer the perfect sacrifice that would save the world from being a place where people were lost and had no hope. He decided that His own son could stand in proxy for the sin-filled world, taking all sin upon Himself.

So, Jesus came, born of a virgin, to save this dying world. He walked on this earth for 33 ½ years, doing the work of His Heavenly Father. At the appointed time, He died by way of crucifixion upon a cross at Calvary, on Golgatha's hill. He shed his blood and died for you and for me. Because His blood was pure, it paid the penalty for all unrighteousness and gave those who believe in Him direct access to His father's throne.

Scripture tells us in Matthew 27:51 that the veil of the temple was ripped in two from top to bottom, at the moment that Jesus' spirit left His body. As a result of the veil's removal, we are no longer required to have a high priest make intercession for us. We, as the children of the Most High God, are able to approach the throne God for ourselves, and Jesus sits on the right hand of the Father making intercession for us.

But what is even more miraculous than God offering His own son as the perfect sacrifice was the fact that when Jesus was placed in grave clothes and placed in a tomb, He only remained there until the third day. God would not have it that His son would remain in the heart of the earth forever. In order for people to believe in the awesome power of God and His dear son Jesus, a miracle had to be performed. So, on the third day, after Jesus died on the cross, He was resurrected, demonstrating the omnipotence of God. This very act was the act that would cause people to believe in a god that reigns supreme and holds the power of the universe in His very hands, a god that could save them from themselves.

Today, if you are an unbeliever, you can change your destiny. You can change where you will spend your eternity. Our Heavenly Father gives us the freedom of choice about how we want to live our life here on earth and how we want to spend eternity. In Deuteronomy 30:19, God boldly declares, *"I call heaven and earth to record this day against you, that I have set before you life and death, blessing and cursing: therefore choose life, that both thou and thy seed may live."*

So, dear friend what choice will you make today? Will you spend your eternity with the Creator or will you suffer Hell's eternal flames? Again, the choice is yours. Just as the men aboard the ship who were with Jonah became believers, you too can make a choice to accept the only one and true living God as your god.

If after reading the above passages, you have decided that you want to spend your eternity in Heaven with God, the creator, and His son Jesus, and the Holy Spirit, read through what has affectionately come to be known as the Roman's Road. This is the road to salvation. As you read through the scriptures that comprise the Roman's Road, you will also read the explanation for each scripture so you will have clarity about what you are reading and confessing.

The Roman's Road to Salvation

The road to salvation begins with Romans 3:23 which declares, *"For all have sinned, and come short of the glory of God."* This scripture explains that everyone has come short of God's glory and needs redemption. Then Romans 6:23a states, *"For the wages of sin is death."* Here, we learn that the consequence of living a life of sin is death. Everyone will experience physical death as a result of the sin committed in the garden of Eden, but those who commit themselves to a life of sin will suffer eternal damnation in the lake of fire (Rev. 19).

Continue with the rest of verse 6:23 that says, *"but the gift of God is eternal life through Jesus Christ our Lord."* There is an alternative to suffering eternal damnation. We can accept the gift of salvation by accepting Jesus as our personal lord and savior. Then, Romans 5:8 says, *"But God commendeth his love toward us, in that, while we were yet sinners, Christ died for us."* We are able to receive the gift of salvation because Christ came to earth and shed His blood for us on the cross.

Continue to Romans 10: 9-10 which says, *"That if thou shalt confess with thy mouth the Lord Jesus, and shalt believe in thine heart that God hath raised him from the dead, thou shalt be saved. For with the heart man believeth unto righteousness; and with the mouth confession is made unto salvation."* If we confess with our mouths that Jesus is the son of God, that he came and died for our sins, and that God raised Him from the dead, we will receive salvation.

Finish with Romans 10:13, which states, *"For whosoever shall call upon the name of the Lord shall be saved."* Call upon the name of God by saying these words, **"Lord Jesus, come into my heart and save me Lord. I believe that you are the Son of God who came and died on the cross for my sins. I believe that you rose from the** grave. I also believe that you now sit in heaven on the right side of the Father, making intersession for me. I accept you as my Lord and my Savior."

Now that you have confessed with your mouth that Jesus is the son of God and that He died for our sins and rose from the grave, **YOU ARE NOW SAVED!!!!** You will spend your eternity in heaven.

The next step is very important- you must find a bible-based church that teaches the word of God and confesses the Lord Jesus Christ to be the son of God. Don't delay. Do this immediately. Do not leave yourself open to the enemy. Get connected with the saints of the Most High God and keep yourself covered with the unspotted blood of the lamb.

Here is my prayer for you.

Father God,

I thank you for the opportunity to minister your word to the unsaved, the unchurched, and the uncommitted. Father God, I pray now for the souls who have just received the gift of salvation. Lord Father, they have opened their hearts to you, and I know that you have received them into your kingdom and written their names in the Book of Life. Father God, I pray that you will touch their lives and show yourself mightily before them. Let their eyes be opened by the scales falling off, allowing them to see clearly.

Father God, I even pray for the backslider, those who have turned away from you after receiving the gift of salvation. You said in your word that you desire that none would perish. So Lord, I send your word to them right now praying that they would confess the iniquity in their heart, repent, and turn from their evil ways, so that they may receive a life of abundance. You said in your word in Matthew Chapter 14, that every knee shall bow before you and every tongue will confess that Jesus is Lord.

Father God, I pray now that we all come under subjection to your word and that we will humbly submit our lives to you. I ask all these things in the name of my Lord and Savior Jesus Christ. Amen, Amen, Amen!!!!

I will continue to pray for your success in your walk with God. Remember, this spiritual walk that you are about to embark on will not be an easy walk, but remember, the race is not given to the swift but to those who endure to the end.

Be blessed with heaven's best. I love you!

A Mother's Heart

Edited by: Dr. Cassundra White-Elliott

A Mother's Heart II

Edited by Dr. Cassundra White-Elliott

A
Mother's
Heart
III

Edited by: Dr. Cassundra White-Elliott

The Mosaic

(A Compilation of Short Stories)

Edited by *Dr. C. White-Elliott*

The Mosaic II

Edited by *Dr. C. White-Elliott*

The Mosaic III

Edited by Dr. C. White-Elliott

THE MOSAIC IV

A Compilation of Short Stories

Edited by Dr. Cassundra White-Elliott

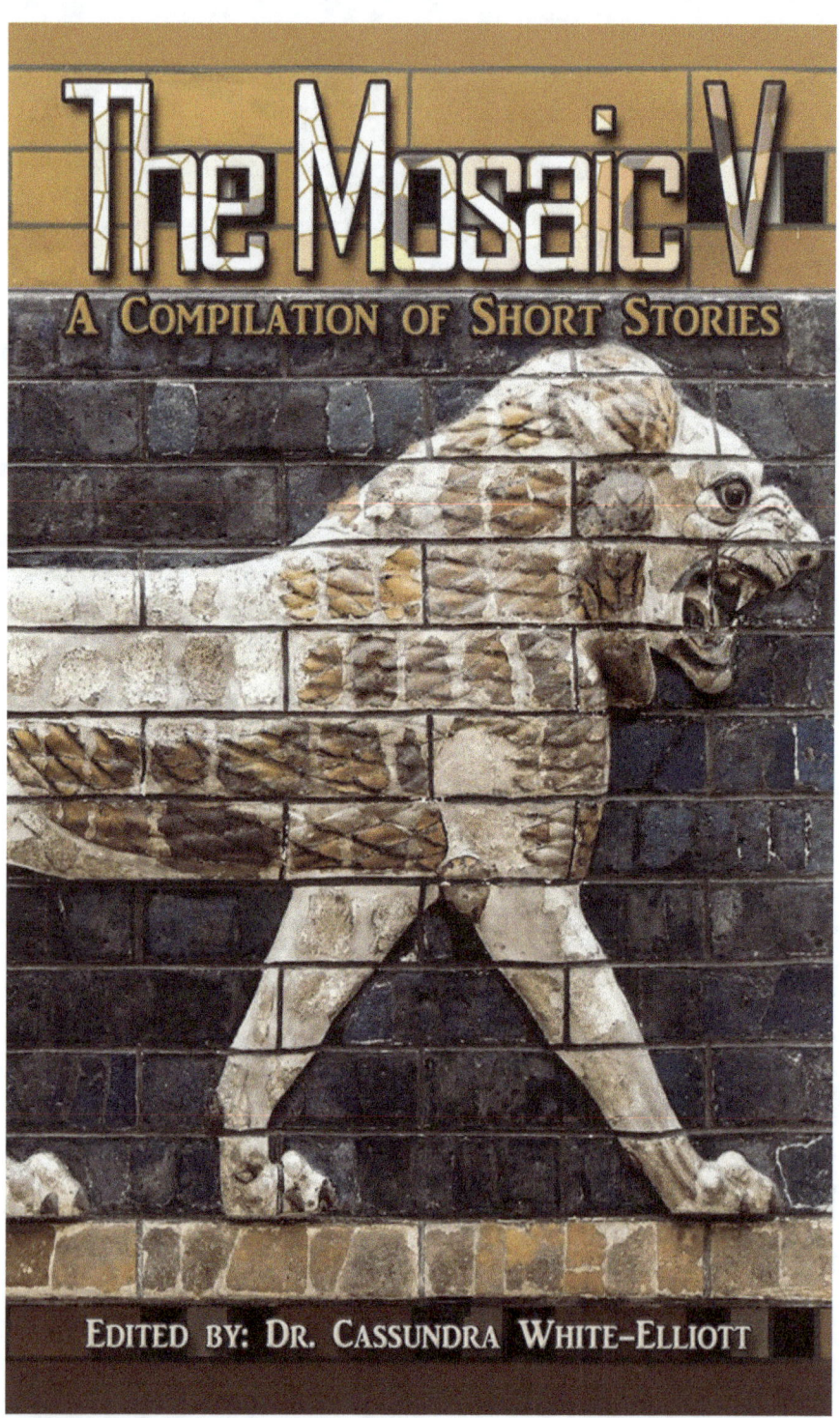

The Mosaic V

A COMPILATION OF SHORT STORIES

EDITED BY: DR. CASSUNDRA WHITE-ELLIOTT

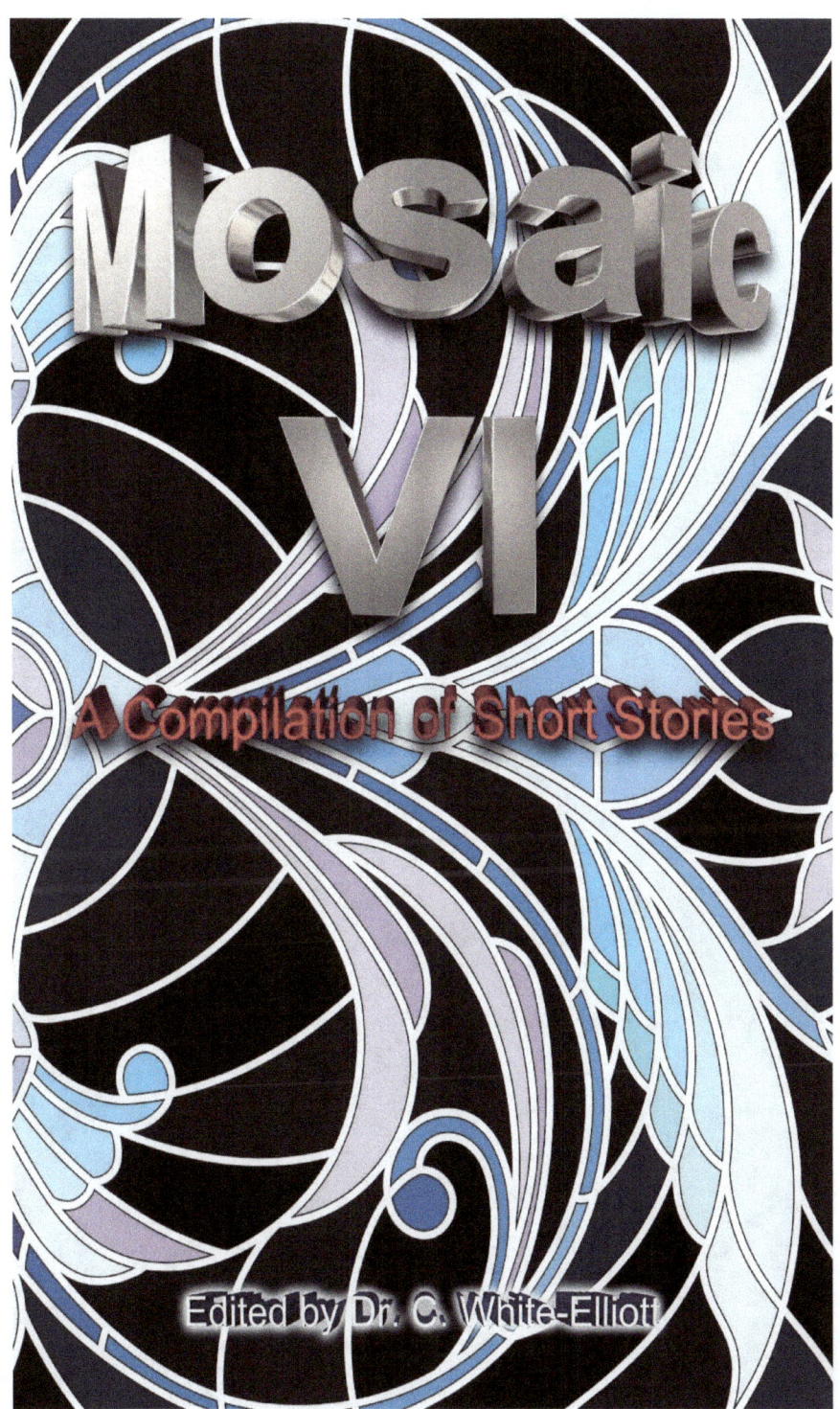

Mosaic
VI

A Compilation of Short Stories

Edited by Dr. C. White-Elliott

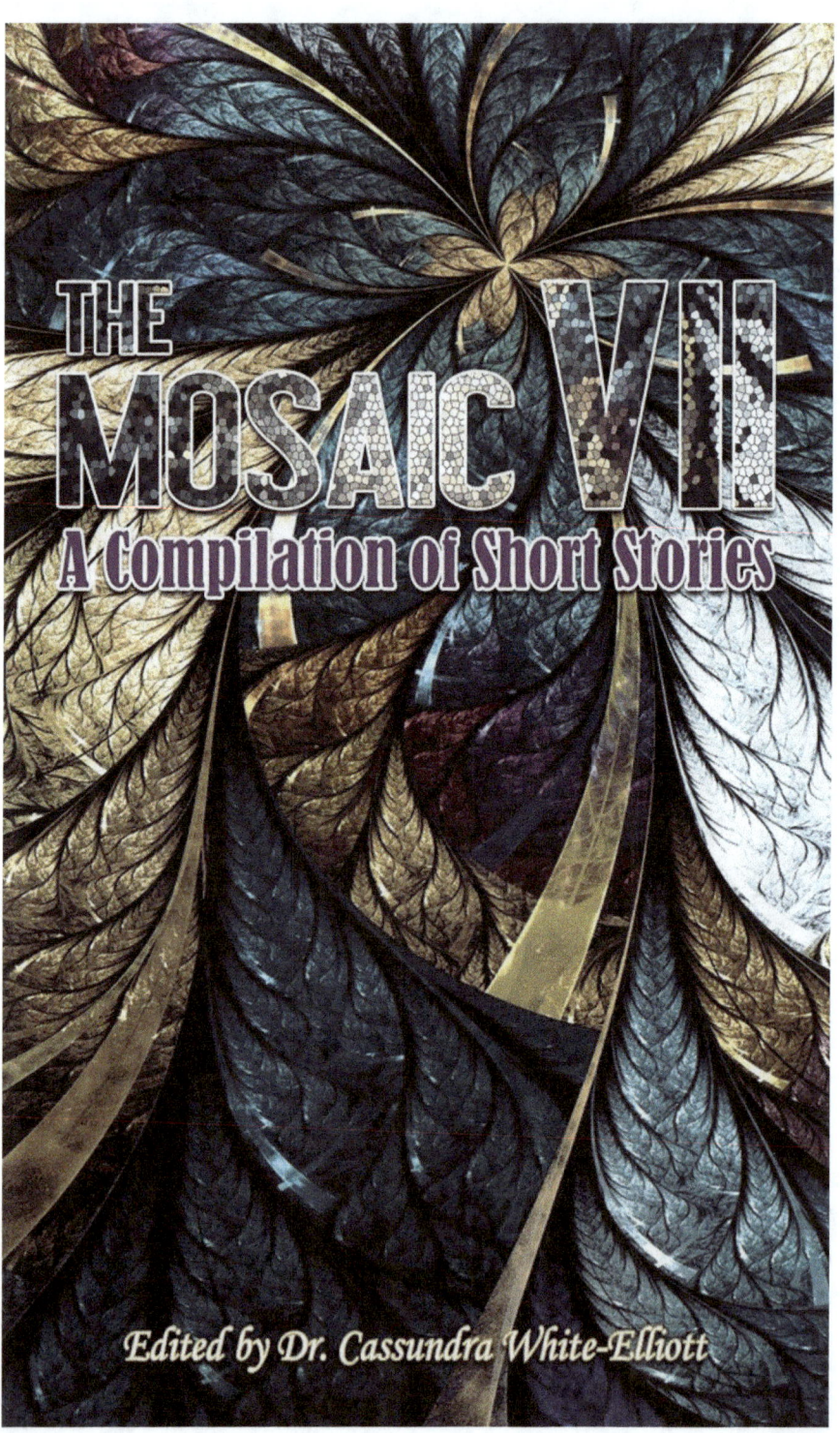

THE MOSAIC VII
A Compilation of Short Stories

Edited by Dr. Cassundra White-Elliott

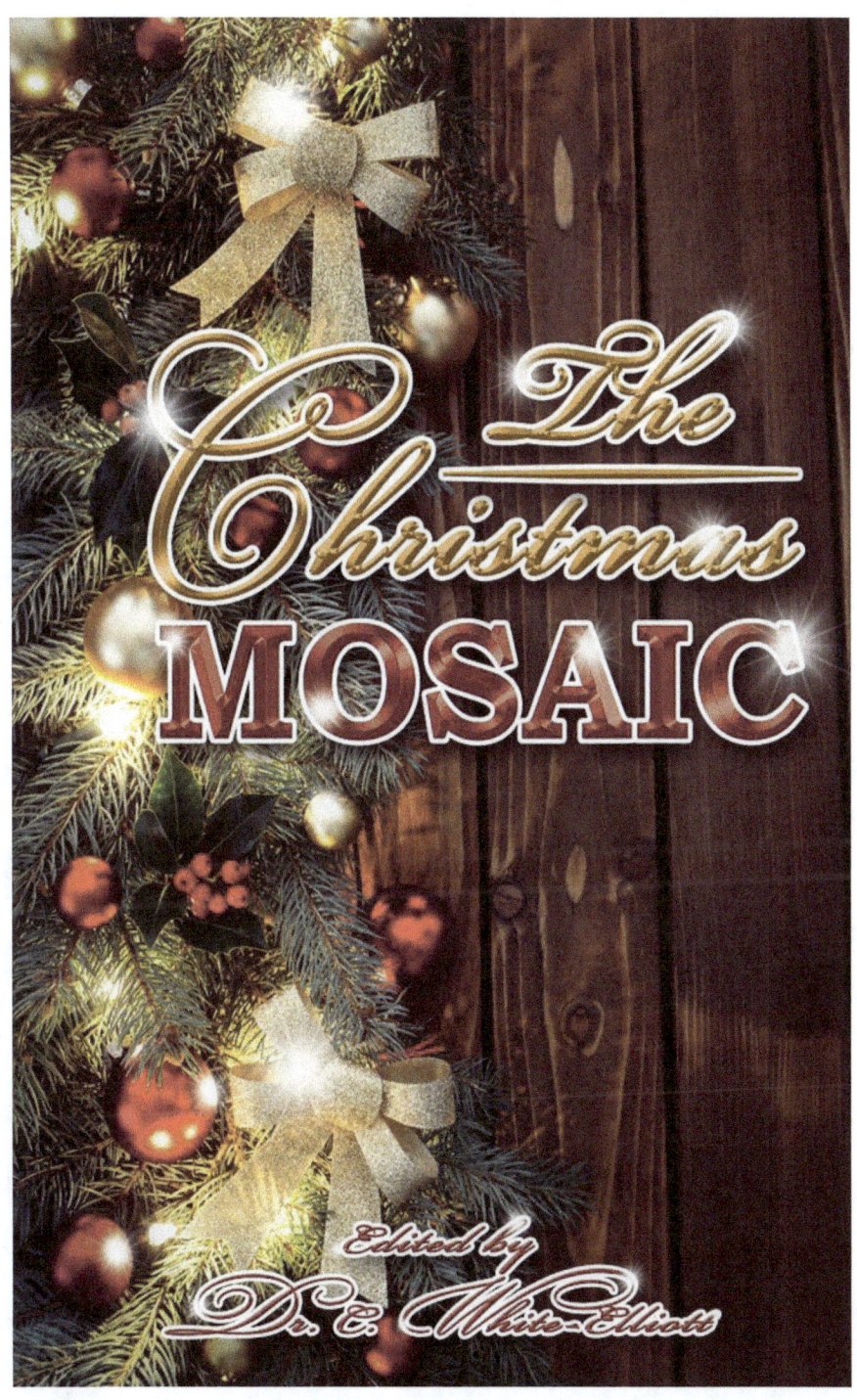

The
Christmas
MOSAIC

Edited by
Dr. E. White-Elliott

The Christmas
MOSAIC II

Edited by Dr. Cassundra White-Elliott

Edited by *Dr. C. White-Elliott*

All Mosaics and A Mother's Heart compilations can be purchased on amazon.com and barnesandnobles.com. Thank you for your support.

www.ingramcontent.com/pod-product-compliance
Lightning Source LLC
Chambersburg PA
CBHW051835020726
47502CB00005B/1802